THE
DESERT KING'S
VIRGIN BRIDE

THE DESERT KING'S VIRGIN BRIDE

BY

SHARON KENDRICK

MILLS & BOON®
Pure reading pleasure

First published in Great Britain 2007
Large Print edition 2007
Harlequin Mills & Boon Limited,
Eton House, 18-24 Paradise Road,
Richmond, Surrey TW9 1SR

ISBN: 978 0 263 19480 7

Set in Times Roman 17¼ on 20 pt.
16-0907-44686

Printed and bound in Great Britain
by Antony Rowe Ltd, Chippenham, Wiltshire

CHAPTER ONE

'MALIK, I'm…' There was a slight pause as Sorrel struggled to push the words out. She cleared her throat and tried again—forcing a smile which felt as if it was slicing her face in two. 'I'm leaving you,' she said, and then wished she could have bitten the words right back, wondering why the *hell* it had come out like that.

Malik looked up from the document he had been reading and a spark of undisguised irritation flashed from his black eyes. Eyes which had been described by the press as cold, or intimidating, or even—in the more colourful publications—as being like those of a lithe predator, about to strike its helpless victim. 'What?' he questioned impatiently.

'I mean…' Sorrel stared at the dark-skinned Sheikh, sitting in his shimmering silken robes at his desk. He had barely noticed her entering the room and he was barely looking at her now—and worrying about how her words had been interpreted was obviously a complete waste of time, since he obviously hadn't been listening either! 'That I'm leaving Kharastan,' she finished huskily.

A frown creased Malik's olive brow—for he was too preoccupied with affairs of state to have heard her. More importantly, he had no desire to bother himself with the internal domestic squabbling of the palace. Surely she knew that? 'Not now, Sorrel,' he growled.

Not *now*? If ever Sorrel had needed confirmation that she was doing the right thing, then it came in the Sheikh's moody and offhand response to her. He spoke as if she was a troublesome fly who had buzzed into his large office suite and he was just about to carelessly swat it.

Amber sunlight slanted in through the

window, turning the sumptuous apartment into a tableau of pure gold and illuminating the man who sat at the desk like some glorious living statue. As always, just the sight of him made Sorrel's heart yearn—but the sooner she got out of the habit of doing *that* then the sooner she would recover from the impact of his potent charm. Instead, Sorrel tried very hard to ignore his physical attributes, and fixed him with a questioning look instead. 'When, then? When *can* we discuss it, Malik?'

'Look!' Impatiently, he waved his hand at the large pile of paperwork awaiting the royal stamp and the royal signature. Beside them lay his open diary, crammed with engagement after engagement. 'You know that there is an important border issue with Maraban which needs to be resolved quickly—and I have a new ambassador to welcome later this morning. Can't you see how busy I am?'

'Yes, Malik,' she said, with a sigh. 'Of course I can see.' It hurt that he should even ask—for surely he must know that she always had his interests at heart? Once, she had been alone in looking out for Malik—in the days when he had been nothing more than the Sheikh's most valued and trusted aide—but now all eyes were fixed on him.

In the royal palace—and in the desert lands beyond—he was the centre of the universe. To be a desert king was considered irresistible in the eyes of the world. When Malik said 'jump', people leapt—usually with a smarmy and obsequious smile pinned to their faces.

It hadn't always been that way, of course. Malik was a late starter in the royal game—he hadn't even realised that he was the illegitimate son of the Sheikh until two years ago, when the bombshell announcement had been made. The old ruler had died, and Malik had been crowned—from aide to king in a simple ceremony—from commoner to royal in an instant. And yet Malik seemed to have adapted to his new status like a falcon which took its first solo flight in the desert sky.

His always haughty air had become fine tuned—but now he had developed a cool dismissiveness towards others. The practical side of Sorrel's character acknowledged that he needed distance—literally, to stop anyone from getting too close to him and to attempt to claw back some of his most precious commodity: time.

Yet, deep down, hadn't Sorrel been hoping that in her case he might make an exception? Didn't it occur to him that she was itching to tell him of her decision and to get on with it— to start making something of her own life, instead of just existing as some invisible satellite of his? No, of course it didn't!

Ever since Sorrel had known him Malik had been an autocratic and supremely dominant man—but since he had inherited the Kingdom of Kharastan his pride and his arrogance had known no bounds. His wishes were always paramount—nothing else mattered except what the Sheikh wanted—and Sorrel had come to the heartbreaking conclusion that there was simply no place for her in his life any more.

Everything had changed—he had, and she had. Suddenly she no longer felt she belonged—certainly not in the land where she had lived most of her life.

Then just where do you belong? The question which had haunted her for so long popped into her head, even though she had been trying to ignore it—because every time she let herself think about it she was frightened by the vision of a great gaping hole in her future.

Malik's black eyes were now scanning the cream parchment pages of his diary and, knowing that he could be seen by none of his servants, he scowled. It was unlike Sorrel to add to the burden of his work.

'There is no appointment for me to see you marked out in my diary.' He frowned, and then he looked up again. 'Did you make one?'

Once, Sorrel might have wanted to weep at such a matter-of-fact statement coming from the man she had idolised ever since she could remember. The man who had in effect 'rescued' her, who had become her legal guardian after the sudden and tragic death of her parents and allowed her to remain in Kharastan instead of being carted off back to England. But this harsh new attitude towards her hurt more than she could have thought possible, and even though she tried very hard to tell herself he wasn't being unreasonable— it wasn't easy.

'No, I didn't make an appointment,' she said flatly.

Malik's eyes narrowed. What was the *matter* with her lately? From being someone he could talk to and relax with, she had become…*edgy*. 'Well, be quick,' he said impatiently, flicking a glance at the modern watch which looked so at odds when contrasted against the fine silk of the flowing robes he wore. 'What is it?'

Sorrel wondered what he would say if she blurted out *I think you've become an arrogant and insufferable pig.* Would he have her taken away for treason?

She flicked her tongue out over lips which had grown suddenly dry. 'I want to go to England,' she said.

'England?' Malik frowned. 'Why?'

'Because...' Where did she begin? Not with the truth, that was for sure.

Because I'm in love with you. I've been in love with you for years, Malik, and you've never even deigned to notice me as a woman.

No, the truth would horrify him. Sorrel had no real experience of men—but the palace library was stocked with the world's greatest literature, and she had read enough classic love stories to realise that she was wasting her time with the black-eyed Sheikh of Kharastan, who had steel for a heart.

'Because I am now twenty-five.'

'No, Sorrel,' he negated. 'You cannot be.'

This was the kind of remark which once she would have found sweet, and amusing—but which now rankled as if he had just insulted her. And in a way he had—for his failure to know her real age went some way towards explaining why he treated her as if she was about six years old.

'I really think that if anyone happens to know how old I am, it's me,' she said, as near as she came to sarcasm with His Mightiness these days.

'Yes. Of course. Twenty-five,' he repeated wonderingly, and for a second he met her gaze full-on. 'How can this be?'

Sorrel steeled her heart against the sudden faraway look in his ebony eyes. A sad, wistful, almost dreamy look—as if he had lost himself in the past.

Which just proved how unrealistically sentimental she had become—*as if* Malik would be longing for the days when he had been just the aide to the Sheikh, instead of the Sheikh himself!

'The years go by more quickly than any of

us realise,' Sorrel said briskly, realising how *prim* she sounded—but that was the trouble: she *was* prim. Basically, the years were zooming by, and with them her youth, and she was wasting it pining for a man who never noticed her. Well, not as a woman.

One day—probably in the not-too-distant-future—Malik would start casting his eyes around for a suitable bride. A woman of Kharastani stock who could provide him with pure-bred Kharastani babies. 'And I can't stay here for ever,' she finished.

'But you don't know England,' objected Malik. 'You haven't lived there for years.'

'Not since I was at boarding school,' Sorrel agreed. 'And even then I didn't what you might call *live* there. Being allowed out to the sweet shop in the village every Saturday morning to spend my pocket money hardly counts as interacting with the country of my birth!'

Malik's hard mouth momentarily softened. He had known her since she was a child—a blonde-haired poppet, as her father had used to call her. And he had been right. Sunny little Sorrel had charmed everyone.

Her parents had been diplomats—clever academics with a hunger for facts and experience which had ended over the treacherous peaks of the Maraban mountain range which bordered the Western side of the country. There, one hot and stormy evening, their plane and their dreams had crashed and lain in pieces on the ground, and the sixteen-year-old Sorrel had been left an orphan.

Perhaps if she had been younger then she would have been unable to refuse to return to her homeland, to be cared for by a distant relative. And if she had been older then there would have been no need for a protector. But she had needed someone, and Malik—a great friend and confidant of her ambassador father—had been named as guardian in their will.

He had been more than a decade older, and in a more liberal country than Kharastan questions might have been asked about whether such an arrangement was appropriate between a teenage girl and a red-blooded single man. But no questions had been asked. Malik's reputation where honour and duty were concerned was unimpeachable. He had overseen her education and her upbringing with a stern eye, far stricter than that of any father—though Sorrel had never given him cause for concern, not even a hint of rebellion.

Until now.

He stared at her. She was almost completely covered in pale silk, as Kharastani custom dictated, so it was almost impossible to known what her figure was really like, though from the drape and fall of the cloth, and the perfect oval of her face, it was easy to recognise that beneath it she was a slim and healthy young woman.

Only a strand of moon-pale hair peeped out from beneath the soft silver lace which covered it, and the only colour which was apparent was the bright blue of her eyes and the natural rose gleam of her lips. For the first time Malik began to realise that somewhere along the way she had become a woman—and he hadn't even noticed.

Should he let her go? 'Can't you just have a holiday in England?' he enquired moodily. 'And then come back again?'

Sorrel sighed. He was missing the point— only she couldn't really tell him what the point was, could she?

'No, Malik,' she said patiently, aware from the sudden narrowing of his eyes that few people said 'no' to him since his sudden elevation in status. 'I've spent my whole life having *holidays* in England—I haven't lived there properly for years. Why, I even went to university here, in Kumush Ay—'

'Which has a fine reputation the world over!' he interrupted, with fierce pride. 'And which enabled you to become possibly the only Western woman to speak fluent Kharastani. Why, you speak it almost as fluently as I do!'

'Thank you.' Briefly, Sorrel bowed her head—aware that the Sheikh had just paid her a compliment and that to fail to acknowledge it would be seen as discourteous. But it was yet another example of how much had changed since his elevation into the royal ranks.

There was a time when she would have playfully teased him—or perhaps challenged him about who was right and who was wrong—but not any more. And the longer you stay, the worse it's going to get, she told herself.

'I don't want to become a stranger to the land of my birth, Malik,' she said fervently. 'And if I leave it much longer then I will be. I'll become one of those people whose only knowledge of their country is through the rose-tinted glasses of memory.'

His eyes glinted as he nodded his black head with slow consideration. 'Yes,' he conceded. 'The ties to our homeland are one of the strongest of all instincts known to man—for they link us to our forebears and make up our very history.'

Sorrel could have kicked the leg of his ornate writing desk in rage, wanting to tell him not to be so damned *pompous*, but she couldn't do that either. He might be speaking to her as if he was aged about a hundred and three, but what he said made sense—and in this instance at least he spoke from the heart. *His* heritage was of huge importance to him, and so he would naturally understand her need to go and investigate *her* roots.

After all, it wasn't his fault that she had stupidly nurtured a rather different fantasy about their shared future over the years…

'Sorrel?'

His voice butted into her thoughts and Sorrel blinked, her heart leaping in spite of everything, the way it always did when he said her name in that uniquely honeyed way of his.

'Yes, Malik?'

'Just what are you proposing to do? In England?'

Try to start a new life. Do the normal stuff

that a twenty-five-year-old woman would have done by now if she hadn't been all caught up with trying to fit in somewhere where she didn't belong. Maybe even find herself a boy-friend along the way.

'I'll look for a job.'

There was a pause. 'A job? What kind of *job*?' he demanded, as incredulously as if she had just started doing cartwheels around the state apartments.

'I can do plenty of things.'

'Oh, really?' He sat back in his chair and, interlacing his long dark fingers in front of the silken shimmer of his robes, fixed her with a piercing black look. 'Such as?'

'I'm a good organiser.'

'That much is true,' he admitted, for she had been co-ordinating palace functions ever since she had graduated. No royal banquet was ever complete without Sorrel quietly ma-noeuvring behind the scenes to prevent delicate egos from clashing.

'And I am also versed in the art of diplomacy.'

He could see exactly where this was leading, and as he was reminded of just how protected and innocent she really was Malik shook his head. 'If you think you'll just be able to walk straight into a job without any formal training, then you are wrong, Sorrel.' Thoughtfully, he drummed one long finger on the polished surface of the exquisite inlaid desk. 'However, I may be able to speak to a few people on your behalf. Perhaps,' he mused, 'I could arrange for you to stay with a family. Yes, that might be the best solution all round.'

'A *family*?'

'Why not? Girls do it all the time.'

Girls, he had said. Not women, but *girls*— and enough really was enough! For the first time in her adult life Sorrel looked around the high-ceilinged palace room and saw it not as a place furnished with priceless antiques and glittering chandeliers and wonderful artifacts but as a kind of elaborate cage. Except that even a bird trapped in a cage could be seen, while she was hidden away like a guilty kind of secret. Prevented from freely mixing with men, covered from head to toe in robes designed to conceal the female form from all eyes. Never before had she minded about the camouflage of the national dress—but lately she had been looking at fashion sites on the internet with a yearning which surprised her.

'I am not a g-girl,' she said, her voice shaking with an emotion she wasn't sure she could identify—even if she had been in the mood for analysis. 'I am a *woman*—not some teenage *au pair* who needs looking after.'

Malik's eyes were caught by the sudden trembling of her lips and his pupils dilated—for it was as if he had never seen them before. Like petals. Provocative and rosy. Did she have any idea what Western men might do when confronted with a pair of lips like that? He glared at her.

'I would feel happier if I knew that you were in capable hands,' he said stubbornly.

It wasn't easy, but Sorrel knew that she had to start standing up for herself if she wanted any kind of independent life. 'Strangely enough, this isn't about *you*, Malik—this is about *me*, and my life. We've been dealing with yours non-stop ever since you became Sheikh, haven't we?'

For a moment he stilled, every instinct alerted to the presence of something he wasn't used to—at least, never with Sorrel—and that something was discord. Black eyes gleamed. Was she daring to *criticise* him? Or to imply that she was not happy with her lot?

His hard mouth flattened into an implacable line of anger which Sorrel had seen before— many times—but never directed towards her.

'Well, do forgive me if you've been *bored*,' he said, in an arrogant drawl which disguised the outrage he felt. Ungrateful little Westerner! He had willingly taken her under his wing, had ensured that she had a stable education and a secure home-life, and she was now throwing back his protection in his face—like some spoilt little child.

How he would like to teach her a lesson!

But as he felt the blood fizzing heatedly through his veins, Malik rose quickly from his desk, momentarily confused by his reaction— if such a state could ever have been said to exist in a man who was a stranger to the very concept of self-doubt. Why, for a moment back then…

Aware that her eyes followed him, he walked over to the window—his back ramrod-straight as he stared out into the manicured grandeur of the palace gardens— and stifled a sigh. When had he last had the freedom to just wander around its scented splendour—without a care in the world?

Not since his last few innocent days as a free man—before the announcement that he was the eldest of the late Sheikh's three illegitimate sons and that the crown of Kharastan was to be placed on *his* head.

In many ways Malik had been well-prepared

for the very specific burdens of kingship, for he had been the trusted aide to Sheikh Zahir for many years, and was well-versed with the intricate customs of the Kharastan court.

But knowing something as an advisor—no matter how highly favoured—was completely different from *becoming* the ruler, especially with very little prior warning. Malik had known that the changes would be much more subtle and far-reaching than the mere swapping of roles.

Gone was the relaxed status he had simply taken for granted. Suddenly he had been hurled into a world where he was no longer able to express an opinion without first carefully thinking it through. For his words would be seized on—twisted around, or analysed for a meaning he had not intended. Yes, he had been able to turn to Fariq—his own assistant—and elevate him to the position of Sheikh's aide, but Malik still felt as if he was on trial. As if he had to prove to everyone—to his people and the world and to *himself*—that he was capable of shouldering this mighty responsibility of power.

Only with Sorrel had he not had to bother—and yet now there was to be another change, and Sorrel wished to leave.

He turned round again to find her eyes wary. And something in that fearful look shook him—seeming to click reality into sudden focus. As though the trepidation in her big blue eyes emphasised more than anything else had done to date just how different his life had become.

She who had never looked on him with anything other than serene and smiling acceptance was now surveying him as if he were some cruel sultan who had stepped out of the pages of the *Arabian Nights*—he, Malik, who had shown her nothing other than kindness!

Well, let her go! Let her see how she enjoyed an anonymous existence in England!

But he saw the faint clouding of her eyes and he relented, giving her one last opportunity to see sense. 'A role could be found for you at the Kharastani Embassy,' he mused.

'I...realise that.'

He heard the unspoken reluctance in her voice, and with anyone else he would have quashed any further enquiry—but this was *Sorrel*, for mercy's sake, who as a child had brought him back a little box covered in seashells from a place called Brighton. 'You do not wish for any assistance?' he questioned proudly.

Sorrel hesitated—for the very last thing she wished was to insult his honour. Kharastani customs were incredibly complex, and it had taken her a long time to understand that the possibility of an offer was always suggested before an offer was made. Thus, the possibility could be rejected and not the offer itself, ensuring that nobody's pride would be hurt.

'I just think it's better if I do it myself. Stand on my own two feet, for the first time in my life.' She turned her face up to his beseechingly, but his eyes were as cold as stones. 'Surely you can understand that, Malik?'

'I think you forget yourself,' he remonstrated cruelly. 'It is not my place to understand one of my subjects—nor theirs to suggest that I should!'

He drew his shoulders back and iced her a look, and Sorrel could have wept—for never in a million years could she ever have imagined Malik pulling rank on her. And *was* she one of his subjects? Perhaps she was—technically, at least.

Once again, the sensation of being enclosed and trapped enveloped her like a velvet throw.

'No, of course it isn't,' she responded stiffly, momentarily lowering her eyes—not so much in a mockery of submission but more so that he would not see the fury reflected in her eyes. When she looked up again, she had composed herself—enough to even curve her lips in a polite little smile. 'Then I shall make the necessary arrangements.'

'Indeed,' he said, deliberately cold and unhelpful, picking up his golden pen in a gesture which was obviously intended to dismiss her.

But Sorrel was not prepared to be so pushed aside—not any more. For Malik himself had just demonstrated how he rewarded loyalty and un-swerving affection—with disdain and contempt.

'I believe that there was a little money set aside in a trust for me by my father?'

He stared at her, tempted to use his power as trustee of her late father's estate. Let her see how long she would last in the world if she had to go out and earn her living like other mortals—*then* she might appreciate her cosseted life within the walls of the palace!

But Malik was not foolish, and he would no more seek to deny Sorrel what was rightfully hers than he would contain her in a place of which she had clearly grown tired. Just a few minutes ago he himself had shuddered at the sensation of being trapped—so why would he inflict it on someone else?

Because he would miss her?

His mouth hardened. Perhaps for an instant, but no more than that—in the way that you might miss your favourite horse if you went to live in the city and found you could no longer ride. But doubtless Sorrel would visit Kharastan from time to time. He would watch her blossom as she embraced her new life— and that was exactly as it should be.

'Yes, Sorrel,' he said, surprised by the sudden heaviness in his voice. 'The money your father left in trust for you was invested by the financial advisors of the late Sheikh.' He paused for emphasis, to let the words sink in, but also to gauge her reaction. 'Thus the amount he left has grown considerably.' He saw her eyes widen, and he knew that he must move quickly to quash any ill-founded dreams that she might have. 'That does not mean that you are now a wealthy woman—but that there is adequate provision for you. I advise you to spend it wisely—cautiously, even—until you are used to dealing with money.'

Sorrel stared at him. What did he think she was going to do? Blow it on hundreds of pairs of shoes or start buying diamonds? 'Thank you for your advice,' she said stiffly.

Malik relaxed slightly. So she was prepared to listen to him! 'Shall I have one of my people talk to you—guide you through all the possibilities of budgeting?'

For a moment Sorrel was tempted—and then some dormant streak of rebellion sprang out of nowhere. All her life, people had 'guided' her and helped make her decisions—and that didn't happen to other people of her age. Why, how many other young women had never paid any rent, nor shopped for groceries—or had to cook their own supper? And were *they* given the benefit of the palace's financial advisors?

Besides, what advice could they possibly give that was going to be relevant to her new life in England? They could hardly tell her how to make savings on the central heating bill!

'Thank you, Malik—but no. I would prefer to stand on my own two feet.'

His eyes narrowed. 'How stubborn you can be sometimes, Sorrel,' he said softly.

'It isn't stubbornness, Malik—it's called independence.'

He hesitated, and then asked the question, knowing that by doing so he was breaking protocol. 'You don't want my help?'

Sorrel shook her head, and as she did so she felt her veil shimmer around her shoulders. She had worn it for as long as she could remember, and yet soon the veil would be lifted and removed—her head bare in a way which was considered unseemly here. It would be freedom in more ways than one—and most important of all she wanted to be free of this one-sided adoration she felt for the Sheikh.

'I want to do it my way.' She should have felt excitement, but at that moment she felt the clammy clamping of fear around her heart as she looked up into Malik's hard black eyes, realising that despite everything she wanted his blessing—his assurance that her actions would not damage their friendship. That once she had got him thoroughly out of her system a residual affection would remain. 'If that's okay?'

He shrugged, deliberately disdainful. 'Do as you please, Sorrel,' he said coldly, and picked up one of the documents he had been working on in a gesture which said quite clearly *I wash my hands of you.* 'But if you don't mind—I think we have exhausted the subject, don't you? And I happen to be rather busy.'

Sorrel stared at him. She had been dismissed as he would a servant, and she had to bite back her rage and her pain as he deliberately bent over his work. Yet somehow she kept silent, her head held high as she walked towards her apartment, telling herself that his reaction to her news after a lifetime of friendship was nothing less than *shameful*.

Well, she would show Sheikh High-and-Mighty Malik! She was going to get right out there in the world and start living her life as it *should* be lived!

So why did her heart feel so heavy as she walked into her sumptuous apartment and looked around? At the delicate inlaid furniture and the paintings whose frames gleamed softly with gold. At the row upon row of beautifully bound and rare books she had inherited from her diplomat father. And at the view over the palace gardens—the emerald lawns leading down to a long rectangle of water, with a fountain pluming in feathery display in the distance.

Against the glittering silver surface she could see the flash of the orange-pink feathers of flamingos—birds so fantastic that they looked almost unreal. Wild ducks and geese landed here sometimes, *en route* to the wide Balsora Sea, and many times Sorrel had seen astonishment on the faces of Western visitors—as if they simply couldn't imagine that such a variety of wildlife existed in a land which was dominated by desert. But Kharastan was a land of constant surprises—its beauty and richness and complexity seeped into your bones almost without you realising it, and she was going to miss it.

Sorrel turned away from the window and stared down at the group of photos which sat atop the baby grand piano. Among the old black and white collection of distant relatives there was a wedding-day photo of her parents, and a later shot of the three of them, laughing on a visit to the Balsora Sea—shortly before their death.

Yet one portrait alone dominated her vision, and she picked it up and drank it in, her heart beating fast as she looked at the formal coronation day study of Malik—his beloved face so stern and so determined beneath the heavy weight of his crown and his destiny.

Rogue tears pricked at her eyes, and a feeling of strange apprehension threatened to overwhelm her as Sorrel quickly put the photo down on the piano and turned away.

CHAPTER TWO

'It will not be as you imagine it to be. And people will treat you differently there. Come back to me if ever you are in trouble, Sorrel.'

Those remembered words echoed in Sorrel's ears—the very last words that Malik had spoken to her just before the door of the dark limousine had closed and shut her off from him.

For ever?

Now she was just being ridiculous! Of course she was going to see him again—and she hadn't come all the way to England and fundamentally changed her life around simply to spend her time thinking about Malik, had she?

The problem was that it was difficult *not* to think about him, not to keep comparing her new life in England, which was so different from the way she'd lived in Kharastan. After the enclosed world of an English boarding school and her cloistered life at court, for the first time in her life she was tasting freedom.

It was just that freedom seemed to come with a price…

Recognising that she was lucky to have the funds to do so—she'd begun looking around for somewhere to rent. She had rejected London—on the grounds that it was too big and too busy, and it would probably swallow her up and spit her out again—but she didn't want to sink into obscurity in some tiny little English village.

In the end she'd chosen Brighton, because it was a bustling and beautiful seaside town, and she recalled spending a wonderful holiday there when she'd been a little girl.

She had found an apartment on the seafront—with huge floor-to-ceiling windows which let the most amazing light flood in. It was one of several owned by Julian de Havilland, a very successful local artist, who only let the rooms out to people who had 'good vibes'. Sorrel suspected that the stark and bare layout of the apartment, with only the barest minimum of furniture, would not be everyone's cup of tea—but it was by far and away the nicest one she had looked at.

'I'll take it!' she said, her attention caught by the sunlight dancing on the sea outside the vast windows.

'There's no curtains, I'm afraid,' he said, raking hands which were stained with Indian ink through an already tousled mane of hair.

'Who needs curtains?' said Sorrel lightly, thinking that she would undress in the bathroom, which featured an enormous great boat of a bath and a noisy cistern.

'Are you working in Brighton?' he asked curiously, watching as she ran her fingertips along the edge of the marble fireplace.

'No, I haven't got a job,' she said, and then,

seeing the heightened curiosity on his face and not wanting to come over as some little rich-girl—which she wasn't—and realising that only by working was she going to get to know people, she gave him a bright smile. 'Not yet, anyway. I'm going to have to start looking.'

'What do you do?'

Ah. That was the question. What *did* she do? Sorrel screwed her face up and came up with her one most marketable asset. 'I can speak French. And German.'

'Fluently?'

'Oh, yes.' She was determined to play down her knowledge of Kharastani. Sorrel had already decided that she wasn't going to pub-licise her background—mainly because it wasn't fair to Malik. He was powerful, and he was a king, and while some people might actually think she was fantasising about even *knowing* him she must never forget that others might wish to make his acquaintance for all kinds of reasons. And she could never presume on their friendship by daring to make introductions to him.

Friendship?

Some friendship!

He hadn't bothered replying to her e-mails and neither had he once picked up the telephone, or in any way acknowledged the couple of jaunty postcards she had sent, with a deliberately cheerful tone—as if she was having the most wonderful time in the world with her newly acquired freedom. As if she wasn't missing him and her life in the exotic and complex country which was Kharastan. But she did.

She missed it all like mad—the apricot-soft dawns and the fiery sunsets, the stark beauty of the desert and the warm, scented air of the palace gardens. And didn't she miss her exceptionally privileged lifestyle there, if she was being completely honest? Hadn't she become rather too accustomed to servants who acceded to her every whim? To having her clothes laundered and her meals cooked and served to her? Why, by the time she had left Kharastan she had actually had her *own* aide!

Most of all she missed Malik. The sight of his beautiful mocking face at state banquets—the sound of his rich, resonant voice as he made a speech to welcome visiting dignitaries. She missed the expectation of bumping into him. The thought that at any moment he might suddenly appear—sweeping through the wide, marbled palace corridors with his silken robes swishing and a cluster of aides scurrying in his wake, because his long stride seemed to cover so much more distance than anyone else she knew.

But didn't that speak volumes about how hopeless her longing for him was? If she analysed the actual *substance* of her relationship with him, it was nothing. A few daily snatched glimpses of him and being a member of an adoring audience as he delivered a speech was not a *real* relationship—hardly even a friendship. She sounded more like a starstruck fan than an equal. For she would never be his equal. Not now.

In the years before the bombshell had dropped that he was the true and rightful heir to the Sheikh there had been hope that he might love her back. But he never had and now he never would. Perhaps deep down Malik had always sensed the true magnitude of his destiny, and she had to accept hers. And hers was here. Now. And she must learn to adapt to this completely different way of living.

It was a shock to the system—but one that she needed if she was to achieve any degree of contentment, she decided, as she signed a cheque and handed it over to Julian.

He took it, folded it, and slid it in the back pocket of his jeans. 'Well, if you need a job and you're a linguist, then why don't you try the Alternative Tourist Office?' he questioned, and saw her puzzled look. 'It specialises in places of interest which are off the beaten track—as well as the usual attractions—but they get loads of foreign tourists who don't speak much English. They've got a crazy little office down the road on the seafront.'

'And they're looking for someone?'

Julian grinned. 'They're always looking for someone! They don't pay great money—but the atmosphere's pretty relaxed.'

It certainly seemed that way. The office was situated a mere shell's throw from her apartment, sandwiched between a clothes shop and a wine bar. A few wilting plants sat on the windowsill, and there was free coffee and a pile of magazines with most of the advertisements cut out—plus music playing from a deck in one corner.

Sorrel was asked a fairly basic question in French and given the job on the spot—mornings only and every other Saturday. She would be working with Jane, who had just left university and couldn't decide what to do, and a very good-looking male model called Charlie, who told her he was currently 'resting'.

'Oh, you're always "resting"!' accused Jane, with a giggle.

It was such a relief to be in a friendly atmosphere with people her own age that Sorrel found herself relaxing for the first time since her plane had taken off from Kumush Ay airport.

The job was also so easy that she felt she could have done it with her eyes shut, and when she wasn't working she kept the plants watered and read everything there was to know about Brighton, because she was determined to do well.

And when Jane and Charlie asked she told them simply that she'd been working in the Middle East but had wanted a change—and that was the truth. It was a gentle shoe-in to the working world, yet Sorrel felt incredibly nervous—given that just a few months ago she had been rubbing shoulders with political leaders and queens. Where had that serene and unflappable Sorrel gone? She seemed to have left her behind.

She guessed that her anxiety stemmed from more than just setting out on her own in a land which was like a foreign country to her—it was as if she had to acquire a whole new identity to cope with her new life.

For a start, she had to go out and buy clothes which were suitable for her new appointment, and how strange that felt—not having to follow the strict dress-code of her adopted country which had become second nature to her.

Without her neck-to-ankle silk gowns she felt almost…exposed—even though she wasn't, not really, and certainly not compared to everyone else. She bought a couple of floaty long skirts and a pair of jeans—but the jeans hung disturbingly low on her hips and the T-shirts she wore with both clung to her breasts in a way she was not used to.

But this is England, she reminded herself—not Kharastan.

In fact, the clothes she wore were very modest—especially considering that the weather was blisteringly hot, since England was having the kind of freak summer heatwave which Sorrel would never have anticipated. Even though they left the front door wide open, the office was like an oven—and during the still nights when she lay in bed Sorrel found herself longing for the air-conditioned coolness of the palace at Kumush Ay.

'Aren't you baking, dressed like that?' asked Jane one morning, as flung her handbag down onto one of the desks. 'You're not in the Middle East now, you know—and these little sundresses are much cooler!'

'Yes, they look cooler,' agreed Sorrel, with a slight longing in her voice as she glanced at Jane's bare thighs. 'But my legs are so pale. Not like yours.'

'Didn't you sunbathe in…Kharastan?' asked Jane.

'It wasn't really encouraged,' said Sorrel, with wry understatement.

'Well, my tan isn't real,' confided Jane—and

when she saw Sorrel's blank look she burst out laughing and began rubbing her hands together. 'Oh, *yes*!' she breathed, with gleeful enthusiasm. 'I've always wanted to do a real-live makeover on someone!'

It was an experience that Sorrel would never forget. First came the beauty salon—where fake tan was sprayed all over her. When she emerged, she shrieked with horror at the blotchy, muddy mess her skin presented—until she was assured that the colour would flatten out. Next she had her toenails and fingernails painted in an iridescent shade of rose-pink.

'You've *never* had a pedicure before?' shrieked Jane in amazement.

'Never,' agreed Sorrel, pushing away her nagging feeling of doubt as she tried to imagine what Malik would say if he could see her now, lying back on a leather couch as if she was awaiting a medical examination, while the nail polish dried. He probably wouldn't even deign to comment. She had taken her chosen path and was now a Western woman who could do exactly as she pleased—no longer under his protection or control. And he had moved on, too, eradicating her from his life completely—which presumably was why he hadn't even had the courtesy to reply to her.

Hot tears stung at her eyes and she blinked them away, willing it not to hurt—not *wanting* it to hurt.

But it did hurt—and Sorrel despised herself for feeling a pain that had no justification in reality. Because nothing had gone on between her and Malik—absolutely nothing—except within the fertile planes of her imagination. Not a nod or a glance, nor a snatched look—and certainly never a kiss or even a touch. Sorrel swallowed. That was true. Unless you counted the times when as a child she had been learning to ride and he had first lifted her onto a horse and gently put her feet into the stirrups, Malik had *never even touched her!*

Even at the weddings of his two half-brothers—when the opportunity had been there—he had not danced with her. Much of the time he had been busy—like her—with the sheer mechanics of organising two such fancy functions, but when there had been a lull… No. She frowned in recall.

He had not actually danced with anyone—even though some of the more blatant female guests had been circling him as she had some-times seen vultures circle a fallen leopard amid the blazing waste of desert sands.

So why was she allowing him to clog up her thoughts? And why was she continuing to dream this dream, which should have been growing more distant by the day—not featur-ing in glorious Technicolor in her mind.

It was time to move on, and there were prac-tical ways she could do that. She'd found the apartment and the job—maybe it was time to stop standing on the sidelines of life in her homeland and to embrace the culture as would any other single young woman of twenty-five.

She glanced up at Jane, who was working her way through sample bottles of moisturiser. 'Could we go shopping after work?'

'*Can* we?' Jane giggled. 'I thought you'd never ask!'

Sorrel had never really hit the shops with a credit card before—her parents had not been big spenders, and had actively discouraged what they'd called *the feeding frenzy of consumer spending*. After their death it had simply not occurred to her to shop. While she'd been at the palace all her clothes had been paid for by the Sheikh—and she had discovered that a very generous salary had been paid into her bank account during those years.

So why shouldn't she splurge a bit? Chainstore dresses weren't exactly going to break the bank, were they?

And Jane was like a child who had been let loose in a dressing-up box.

'Try this!'

'No! I can't—scarlet is not my colour,' protested Sorrel.

'How do you know until you've tried it?'

How indeed? To Sorrel's surprise, Jane was right—not only did scarlet suit her, but the little cotton sundress looked rather good when teamed with some clashing orange beads. It was the last thing she would have worn in Kharastan—but surely that was a good thing? New life, she reminded herself. New woman.

In the end she bought four dresses, a denim mini-skirt, and some cool tops—some with teeny spaghetti straps and others with no straps at all—and a pair of vertiginous wedge sandals which made her legs look almost indecently long.

'You'll get a chance to show them off tonight,' said Jane.

Sorrel blinked. Had she missed something? 'What's happening tonight?' she asked.

'You are,' said Jane firmly. 'I'm not asking

any questions, since you obviously don't want to talk about it, but I can tell just by looking at you that you're trying to get over *some bloke*—the only way to do that is to find another one, and that's exactly what we're going to do!'

Sorrel's first impulse was to recoil in horror at the very suggestion. To protest that finding a man was the last thing on her mind—until she began to worry that maybe there was something *wrong* with her. There must be—if she was objecting so strongly. In twenty-five years she had *never* had a boyfriend—never even kissed a man—and how sad was that? But there were some things you didn't confide—and, much as she liked Jane, that was one of them.

She needed to break the cycle of emotional dependence on the man whose affection for her was based on his obligation as her guardian.

Swallowing down her panic, she nodded. 'Where will we go?'

'The wine bar. Tonight—at seven.'

Sorrel got ready, feeling mixed up and a fraud—but knowing that she should be experiencing the sense of excitement she suspected most other women her own age would be feeling if they were wearing brand-new clothes to go for a carefree night out on a hot summer evening. But she felt as if she was outside her own body, looking at herself with the detached eye of an interested observer instead of being the participant.

Part of her was aware that the itsy-bitsy floaty blue dress looked good, and that her blonde hair had never looked so pale or so shiny as it cascaded down her back to her waist. And that her tanned brown legs did look so flattering—especially when she wore them with open-toe sandals which showed off her dazzling pedicure.

There was an extraordinary moment when she walked into the crowded wine bar and every head turned in her direction. She looked behind her—thinking that someone famous must have followed her in. But, no, they were looking at *her*.

'Why is everyone staring?' she hissed at Jane, rubbing her finger underneath first one eye and then the other—in case her supposedly smudge-proof mascara hadn't lived up to the extravagant claims made on the packet.

'Oh, come *on*!' reprimanded her friend acidly. 'You look a knockout—that's why. Charlie—get Sorrel a drink, will you?'

Sorrel accepted the glass of white wine Charlie pushed into her hand and took a sip. And here was another problem. Alcohol was not taken freely in Kharastan—although it was always provided in the palace for foreign dignitaries. But Sorrel had only ever tasted champagne at the royal weddings of Xavier and Giovanni—Malik's two half-brothers—and she hadn't been mad about it. It had made her feel a bit too dreamy on two dangerously romantic occasions, and she had looked up and found Malik glaring at her and had hastily put the glass down.

Well, not any more! Why shouldn't she have a drink like any other person in the civilised world? It wasn't as if she was knocking it back—not like some of Jane's friends.

But a couple of large glasses of rough wine bar plonk was having a profound effect on a someone who wasn't used to drinking and who hadn't eaten anything since lunchtime. The wine bar had started to get hot and stuffy, with smoke drifting in from outside, where all the smokers were gathered, and Sorrel felt herself swaying slightly.

'You okay?' questioned Jane.

'I need to eat something,' said Sorrel woozily.

'Yeah. Me, too. Tell you what—let's get a curry and take it back to your place.'

It seemed churlish to object—especially when Jane had gone out of her way to help her buy clothes—and Sorrel didn't even protest when several of the others they'd been talking to decided to tag along. They seemed a nice, if slightly noisy bunch, and she was going to have to learn about entertaining sooner or later, wasn't she?

In the end, twelve people stumbled into her beautiful flat and took silver cartons of curry into the kitchen—ladling out heaps of yellow rice and chicken in shiny sauces and great wodges of bread. There weren't enough plates to go round, so some people were eating out of cereal dishes and pouring wine into mugs. After they'd eaten someone found a non-stop music station on the radio—and what Sorrel would have loosely described as dancing began.

Jane was swaying with her arms locked around someone whose name Sorrel thought was Scott, though she couldn't be sure, and then another couple flopped down onto one of the sofas and began kissing quite openly. Sorrel started wishing that everyone would leave so that she could go to bed. And what was that sickly sweet smell of the smoke drifting in from the balcony when she had most definitely said that there was to be no smoking?

It should have been wonderful—especially as outside the uncurtained windows the moon was beginning to illuminate the sky with a pale terracotta sheen. But it was the opposite of wonderful—particularly when Scott stumbled up to Sorrel and tried to pull her into his arms.

'Come and dance with me,' he mumbled.

'I can't… Scott, will you please let go? I happen to be holding a plate of curry—' And then the doorbell rang, and Sorrel felt a mixture of relief and alarm at its piercing shrill—relief because it meant that she could extricate herself from Scott's arms, and alarm because she wasn't expecting anyone. She didn't *know* anyone.

Apart from the landlord!

Heart pounding, and a chilly, clammy feeling in her hands, Sorrel put the plate down and made her way out into the hall. When she pulled the door open her knees threatened to give way.

Because there—with a small phalanx of body-guards standing clustered around him—stood the formidable and disapproving figure of Malik.

CHAPTER THREE

FOR a moment Malik and Sorrel just stood staring at one another, and for a couple of moments longer she almost didn't recognise the Sheikh, yet wasn't sure why. But there was no time to deal with that—not when she was having to confront the burning look of rage which sizzled black fire from his angry eyes. His narrowed gaze was sweeping over her dishevelled appearance, and she realised what a sight she must make.

'What is *this*?' he choked, in a disbelieving voice she had never heard him use before.

'Malik—'

But he silenced her with an imperious wave of his hand and a terse command made in

Kharastani as he glanced over her shoulder to the scene behind and flinched as if someone had punched him.

'What is this scene of utter *debauchery*?' he iced, in disgust.

He didn't seem to want a reply to his question, because he uttered a few more terse commands in his native tongue and the burly-looking men who were with him moved quickly into the apartment and took control.

It was like watching a team of soldiers going into enemy territory, Sorrel thought weakly, as she watched one of the guards march over to the radio and silence it. With the cessation of music everyone in the room froze, and then stared in disbelief at the group of dark-skinned men with black eyes and a shimmer of strength about them which seemed so at odds with the men who were partying.

'What the hell?' Scott lurched over towards Sorrel, and she wanted to yell at him to stop, to go away—to not let himself be annihilated by Malik's strength and power.

'Want a hand, baby?' he slurred.

Sorrel could feel the disgust emanating from every pore of Malik's impressive frame as he stepped into the hallway.

'Get rid of him,' he bit out.

She knew that there was no point in arguing with him, and she hoped that Scott and company would have the sense to realise the same.

'Now!' Malik roared.

Scott scuttled away like an insect who had just been revealed beneath a stone.

'Can you all go, please?' urged Sorrel quickly, and she could see that they needed no second bidding as they scurried round to find handbags and shawls which had been deposited around the flat, and then started trooping out.

Only the couple standing smoking the sickly sweet substance on the balcony seemed oblivious to the uproar in the apartment, and Malik's eyes narrowed in their direction before he nodded briefly to one of his guards.

If she hadn't already been panicking about just what Malik would do when the flat was emptied, it would have been almost comic, thought Sorrel, as she watched the guard striding towards them, whereupon he plucked the joint from the woman's fingers and crushed it between his own.

'Call the police!' ordered Malik imperiously.

'Malik, no, please—'

'You have been *taking drugs*?' he hissed.

'*No!*'

'Drinking, then?'

'Two or three glasses, that is all.'

'All?' With an effort Malik steadied himself, sucking in a deep draught of air and only just preventing himself from hauling her into his arms and…and… He watched as the last of the pathetic-looking men shuffled sheepishly from the flat, and then he barked out an order to his guards. In a daze, Sorrel watched as they too disappeared—until it was just her and Malik alone in the flat.

'Shut the door,' he said softly.

'Malik—'

'I said, shut the door.'

There was something in his tone which was making her feel quite peculiar but it was also a tone which broached no argument—and at that precise moment Sorrel felt about sixteen again.

Until she looked into the dark mastery of his eyes and realised that he had never looked at her like *that* when she was sixteen—with a combination of simmering fury and something else which she didn't dare start to analyse, because it was only threatening to make her light-headedness worse.

So she closed the door and then stood looking up at him, a hopeful expression on her face. Maybe he had finished venting his wrath, and now that he had would quietly forgive her.

But there was no forgiveness on the dark, rugged face with its alluring shadows cast by his amazing bone structure—nor in the almost fevered glitter of his ebony eyes. His features were set in a stony mask, and then Sorrel realised what it was about him which had made him look so different when she'd first opened the door.

He was wearing a suit!

Sorrel swallowed. She had never seen him wearing anything other than his traditional robes—which seemed less like clothes and more like an extension of him—and this new and different Malik took a little getting used to. Somehow it made her feel uncomfortable to look at him in such traditionally Western clothing, and at first she couldn't quite work out why.

The pale grey trousers did not exactly cling to the hard sinew of his legs, but they certainly emphasised the muscular length of his thighs—just as the jacket highlighted the broad shoulders and torso, tapering to a narrow waist and hips.

An open-necked shirt gave her the faintest

glimpse of a whorl of crisp black hair at his chest, and Sorrel felt faint as she realised just what it was that was making her feel so uncomfortable—the Western clothes accentuated his masculinity in a way which his Kharastani robes never had. Those merely *hinted* at the body which lay beneath—but now, for the first time ever, she could actually *see* it.

'Look at you,' he said softly, and Sorrel's eyes widened—for it seemed that he was as taken aback by *her* appearance as she was by his. Was he actually going to compliment her? she wondered, as she heard that husky note in his voice. But from the oblique look in his black eyes it was impossible to tell.

He let his gaze rake over her—slowly—in a way he had never done before. But then she had never provided him with the inclination to. Yet the outfit she wore tonight virtually screamed *Look at me*!—so who could blame him if he did?

It was not a Sorrel he recognised—in a dress

that skimmed her tanned thighs, which gleamed faintly like oiled silk, and beneath the filmy fabric he could see the lush movement of her breasts. The shimmer of her hair—like pale, spun gold—cascaded in a gleaming waterfall down her back. But it was not simply the blatant display of her body which had made him stare at her in disbelief—but the make-up which so marred her beauty.

Yes, the sweep of black mascara curving her long lashes made her blue eyes look enormous in her heart-shaped face, and the gleam of lipstick made the petal-softness of her lips even more provocative. But where was her innocent beauty gone?

Had it gone?

Malik felt his heart slam against his ribcage, and a feeling halfway between rage and despair as he moved his face closer to hers.

'So, did you achieve your aim, Sorrel?' he questioned unsteadily.

What riddle was this he was testing her with?

Sorrel wondered. But she wanted to do something—anything—to remove that obdurate look of anger from his face, and so she played along.

'What aim?' she questioned back.

The slam of his heart increased. 'Did you dress like a...*tramp* in order to lose your virginity to the first man who would take you?'

Lose her *virginity*? Sorrel swayed. Only this time it had nothing to do with the wine but with sheer, disbelieving anguish that Malik could utter such damning words of criticism against her and look at her with such contempt.

Fiercely, she bit her lip, and the self-inflicted pain brought her up sharply—what *right* did he have to chastise her in such a way? He had been her guardian, yes, and a remarkably good one for many years. But the years had now passed and his little bird had flown the nest—and she would not be insulted like that for behaving just as any other young woman of the same age would do.

'I am *not* dressed like a tramp!' she defended.

'Really? That is a matter of opinion.' He saw the way her breasts jiggled when she moved—like some damned belly dancer! Controlling his angry breathing only with a monumental effort, he flicked her a disdainful look. 'And you haven't answered my question!'

She stared at him and he stared back, a silent exchange going on between their clashing gazes—his black and accusing and hers indignantly blue. But she was damned if he thought he could quiz her about her innocence. 'And neither do I intend to!'

He sucked in an outraged breath. Did her refusal mean an admission of guilt? But he could not force her to answer—and certainly not when she was standing there wearing…'Just go and change your clothes, Sorrel.'

For a moment she really thought she had misheard him.

'I'm sorry?'

'No, Sorrel—it is too late for apologies,' he ground out.

This was even worse! 'I wasn't *apologising*!' she spluttered. 'I just can't believe this is happening. You storm in here, asking me personal questions, and then you order me to get changed—as if I'm a five-year-old who has spilt paint on her overalls!'

Oh, that she *was* five years old again—she would not be in a position to defy him! What a stupid little fool she was being, he thought furiously. Did she not realise her bare legs and tiny skirt were making him want to…to…? Appalled at the progress of his thoughts, he swallowed.

'Do not play games with me, Sorrel,' he said unevenly. 'Don't you realise the power a woman has over a man when she puts her body on display? Is that what you want? For me to have difficulty concentrating on what I have come to say to you since you are dressed—or rather *un*dressed…' deliberately, he tempered his words '…in such a provocative manner.'

Sorrel blinked. Was Malik actually admitting that he had *noticed* her? Yet could she blame him for his censure? He was judging her by Kharastani standards, which were far stricter than any she had found here, and to be honest the dress was a little short—she had thought so earlier, only Jane had persuaded her otherwise and Sorrel had let her.

For the first time since he had walked in she bowed her head very slightly, in respect of his title and his status. 'Very well,' she said quietly. 'I will go and put on something more… *suitable*—if you would like to make yourself at home, Malik?' It was only as she left the room that she realised what a ridiculous thing it had been to say. As if this was anything *like* his home—the palace.

Once she had gone Malik relaxed—freed from the unexpected physical temptation which the sight of her had dramatically provoked. He shook his dark head, briefly per-plexed—a state that did not sit readily or easily with him—but just as quickly the sensation vanished. It must have been caused by tired-ness—by the unremitting weight of duties which had fallen upon him. And yet…

Unseen by the eyes which usually followed him, Malik allowed his tongue to flick over his lips, moistening their dryness, and then wished he had not—for the action made his body ache. Fiercely he tried to wipe out the image of Sorrel standing there in front of him, all legs and breasts and flowing silken hair—but it wasn't easy.

In his mind she had always been a child, and then a vivacious teenager. She had somehow made a seamless and unseen transition into womanhood, almost without his noticing. The robes she usually wore had helped disguise her very attributes, of course—and wasn't that one of their functions? Not to put unnecessary temptation in the way of men?

He could not be seen with a woman who looked that way, he realised, and for a moment he questioned the advisability of the proposal he was about to make to her. Yes, she had acceded to his request that she put on something more suitable—but what if that was a one-off? What if Sorrel had already embraced her new freedoms with a passion—what if she had changed and moved beyond the behaviour expected of those who associated with the Sheikh of Kharastan?

Malik sighed. It was yet another example of how much was different since he had found out about the accident of birth which had suddenly transformed him from high-ranking royal aide to ruler of a vast and affluent desert nation— with all the joys and burdens which went hand-in-hand with such a responsibility.

His late father, Zahir, had enjoyed a long, dynastic marriage, but his wife had been unable to bear him children. Many in Zahir's position would have taken another wife— instead he had taken lovers, each of whom had borne him a child. His youngest son, Xavier, was half-French. Giovanni was half-Italian.

Only Malik, the oldest, was of pure and true Kharastani blood—his mother a noblewoman who had died in childbirth.

Malik had been a lonely, motherless child who had become the Sheikh's right-hand aide. Yet he had been denied a father—for the momentous discovery of his lineage had come too late for him to enjoy a relationship with the man who had sired him.

Yet as he glanced around the apartment he acknowledged that his solitude had helped to forge his character—to make him the man he was today. In reality, there could have been no better training for the role of king—for to rule was to exist in isolation from other men.

And women.

He walked through into the kitchen, and for a moment he studied the debris there as an archaeologist might study the ruins of some unknown civilisation he had stumbled upon. What lay before Malik now was a scene completely outside his experience.

Food lay congealed in silver containers—some of it spattered on the surfaces—and half-empty bottles stood in warm puddles of beer. In his country food—even when it was simple—was always served with a certain amount of ceremony and respect. Fine wines would accompany meals, if requested, but Kharastani subjects tended to prefer the juice of a pomegranate mixed with crushed limes and mulberries and a spoonful of honey—the beloved concoction which was known as *labbas*.

His eyes flicked to where a spoonful of rice lay coagulating on the side. And now Malik's lips curved with distaste—never in Kharastan would there be such an undignified mess daring to masquerade as entertainment.

Was this what Sorrel had wished for when she'd demanded to leave Kharastan? This the destiny she followed—the dream she chased? This casual and rather depressing sight of excess combined with little elegance or formality?

Abruptly he turned away and walked back

into the large sitting room—though he did not put any of the lamps on. The windows were open to the world, and his bodyguards would have a fit if he did—and besides, it was strangely soothing to look at the room in the moonlight. At least here he could see a certain amount of beauty—mainly provided by the living backdrop of the sea directly opposite. Moonlight danced on the little waves, making them silver and slick. And the sea was the sea….as fundamentally beautiful here in Brighton as it was by the shores of his beloved Balsora where as a child he had learnt to swim—as slippery and as agile as an eel.

He sighed, lost in the non-threatening landscape of the past—where all the rough corners of authenticity could be rubbed away with a little help from the imagination—until a soft and familiar voice broke into his thoughts.

'Malik?'

He turned then, and the breath caught in his throat—like dust.

For Sorrel was standing before him—looking at once like Sorrel, and yet not like her at all. Gone were the over-short dress and the high-heeled shoes which had made her look so outrageously available. Now her shapely body was covered—not with the familiar robes of Kharastan, but with Western clothes which served the purpose almost as well.

A ruffled skirt fell to the ground, worn with some kind of T-shirt—but unlike her traditional garb this top hugged her lush young breasts, emphasising their thrusting curve in a way which was making him hard.

He bit back his despair at the effect her appearance was having on him—aware that this was *his* problem, not Sorrel's, and accepting that perhaps it was time he turned his mind to the delights of the flesh. Not with *her*, naturally, but with someone beautiful and willing and eager to be his lover—someone who would make no demands on him in any way. Because he had allowed pleasure to become a distant memory. He had done nothing but work, he recognised now, ever since the solemn glory of his coronation day. No wonder there had been a chink in his armour—allowing inappropriate thoughts of Sorrel to surface.

Since his accession he had not dared to relax—not for a single moment—afraid that he would be found wanting by a people still reeling from their beloved Sheikh's death and the colourful reality of his private life! And neither had he wanted to fail—to let his people down in any way—so he had put everything into taking over the formidable reins of his kingship.

It was not the kind of role you could ever really be prepared for—no matter how well you knew how the 'job' functioned. Because it was far more than just a job—it was a complete and all-consuming way of life, and it was one which required the very definite stamp of his personality to make it uniquely his. No wonder there had been no time to think of women….

'Is this better?' asked Sorrel softly.

Much better, he wanted to purr, and then, with the iron-hard resolve which had made his enemies and admirers alike dub him Malik the Steely, he let his dark lashes flutter down to partially conceal the hectic glitter in his eyes.

'Is there a room which isn't overlooked?' he demanded. 'Somewhere more private?'

Sorrel's heart began to race—because wasn't this a desire she had nurtured since as long as she could remember? Of the forgiving shadows of the night, with only the romantic glowing disc of a huge moon outside, and Malik there, with her. Only him, and only her…

Yet she was scared. Terrified, even—and her stomach was contracting with the aching conviction that this was what she wanted.

'Malik?' she breathed uncertainly. 'Are you sure?'

'Of course I am sure!' Malik frowned. 'You suggest that we conduct this talk in a room which brazenly omits to have drapes at its vast windows? Allowing time for some sniper to take a pot-shot at me?'

Thank heavens for the dim light which hid her blush of shame from him. How could she have got it so very wrong?

'Oh, Malik,' she whispered, and her heart turned over as she thought of the selfish nature of her thoughts when compared to the mortal danger at which he hinted. Was that how shallow and selfish she had become? 'Is that…*likely*, then?'

He gave an impatient shake of his dark head. 'It is not a *probability*,' he said shortly. 'But it is always a *possibility*.' And besides, a slightly scaremongering tactic might help click her onto another kind of wavelength—one which could entertain all kinds of scenarios which simply would not have happened if they had been on home territory, back in Kharastan. Because she needed to think differently if she was to be part of his plan.

A plan about which he had still mentioned nothing!

'Please,' she said quickly. 'I know where we can go.'

Having demanded somewhere more private, he could now hardly back out of it—but he prayed that it was not a bedroom. To his relief and perplexity, it was not.

'The bathroom?' he questioned in disbelief, as she snapped on a switch which illuminated a circle of lightbulbs set in theatrical style around a mirror.

'I know it isn't….conventional.'

'You can say that again,' said Malik faintly, but for the first time in weeks a brief smile curved his lips.

'But look—it's windowless. Unobserved.' And she needed to repair the damage of earlier, to put their relationship back in its proper box. To try to convince herself that it felt as easy and as relaxed with him as it used to.

'Yes. So it is.' Malik looked around, taking in the clutter of the room, aware with a sudden poignant pang that this feminine intimacy— which would be the habitat of most men, once they married—would never be his. He let his keen gaze commit the whole scene to memory—all the bottles lining the windowsill, along with candles and a curved glass jar of something coloured green which he assumed was destined for her bath.

Her bath.

Malik swallowed as once again he was haunted by that insistent pulse—beating re-lentlessly at his temple and now throbbing deep within his groin, too. Why the hell had she brought him in *here*?

Because she was following his orders!

And it was time he assumed the upper hand.

'I cannot talk in here,' he snapped—his sweeping hand movement managing to convey his disdain and incredulity that he had ever allowed himself to be lured into such an unsuitable setting in the first place. 'Have you eaten?'

Food had been the very last thing on her mind, and in truth she hadn't had a thing— mainly because he had burst in with all his guards before she'd managed to get a forkful of curry into her mouth. Sorrel shook her head, and Malik slid a phone from his pocket, punched out a number and issued a curt directive to the person who answered immediately.

'Bring the car round, would you?' he said, his black eyes fixed to her face. 'And reserve a table for two for dinner.'

CHAPTER FOUR

SORREL had forgotten what it was like to be a part of royal life—to be whisked along by its smooth and efficient machinery. There were never any blips when you were with a king—or if there were, then you were shielded and protected from them.

Cars turned up when they were supposed to, and no traffic jams ever impeded progress—since roads were cleared just to make the journey trouble-free. Planes took off on time, trains ran to within seconds of their predicted timetables, and tables in restaurants magically became available at a moment's notice—no matter how exclusive the eatery, nor how crowded.

At the exact moment that Sorrel and Malik

stepped out of her apartment block, a limousine with tinted windows slid to a halt. It moved with all the importance and weight of a heavily bullet-proofed vehicle, and of course it demonstrated to Sorrel the downside of a privileged and royal life.

Sorrel hadn't put up any objections when Malik had 'suggested' they eat out—not just because her stomach was empty, but because she knew it would be pointless to argue with him when he was in this kind of mood. And perhaps because she could see his point, that the ruler of Kharastan could not be expected to have an unchaperoned conversation in a single woman's bathroom!

He still hadn't given her any clues about what it was he wished to say to her.

'So what's this talk you want to have with me?' she asked, forcing a casual note into her voice that she was far from feeling as she slid onto the car seat next to him.

Malik's black eyes glittered her a warning.

Had she always spoken to him so freely, he wondered, or had he simply forgotten? Certainly there was no other person than Sorrel in his court who would have dared address him in such a blasé manner. And since she had left Kharastan he seemed to have become aware of the starchy formality of his life as never before.

Yet he was momentarily distracted by the faint outline of her leg through the filmy material of her skirt, and the subtle fragrance of the perfume she wore, and he leant back against the soft leather of the seat so that he could avert his gaze without appearing to do so. 'I do not intend to discuss it here and now,' he cautioned coolly. 'You must wait until we get to the restaurant.'

Oh, *must* she? Once she might have bristled at the rather *pompous* way he was speaking to her, but Sorrel was still feeling unsettled—as much by the way he had been looking at her back there as by the unexpectedness of his appearance. And now they were closeted together in the back of a limousine and suddenly it felt *different*. Awkward. As if the old ease which had always existed between them had somehow been obliterated and replaced with something darker—something she didn't recognise and wasn't sure she wanted to.

Swallowing down her nerves, she started to make conversation, as she had done innumerable times with visiting diplomats to the palace, but never with Malik. 'So where are we going?' she asked, because talking distracted her from the awareness of his male heat and his hair, which gleamed like the wing of the Black Kite which flew so powerfully over the desert sands.

'Does it matter?' he queried carelessly.

'Bet it's the Etoile de la Mer,' she hazarded, and then, in answer to his questioning look. 'It's the best hotel in Brighton.'

'You have visited it before, perhaps?'

She hesitated, wondering if she could possibly convey how different her life here was from the privileged existence she'd enjoyed in Kharastan. 'Hardly. It isn't really in my price league.'

'No? I'm sure that there must be a queue of men eager to take you out for an expensive supper, Sorrel,' he murmured silkily.

His soft words made it abundantly clear what he thought those men might be granted as a reward for such an expensive supper, and Sorrel was conscious of his insulting implication. Yet she was also aware that it would be an unforgivable breach of protocol to risk the driver hearing her snap back a comment at the Sheikh, and so she merely allowed her mouth to curve into an enigmatic smile.

'Yes,' she agreed dreamily. 'A queue that stretches right round the block and back again.'

'This is true?' he hissed.

The look she sent him was one of pure challenge, sparking blue from her eyes. 'Wait until we get to the restaurant,' she retorted softly, replicating his own words. 'I do not intend to discuss it here and now.'

There was a short and disbelieving pause as he registered her insolence, and Malik felt his blood on fire with an unfamiliar heat. He felt himself hardening beneath his robes, cursing the sweet-painful throb of desire, and silently cursed that it had been Sorrel who had brought him to such a point and at such an inconvenient time.

If it had been any other woman he would have slipped his hand beneath her skirt. Would have tapped sharply on the driver's window and alerted him to the fact that he had changed his mind. That he was no longer hungry. Well, not for food. But it was not any other woman. It was…

'Malik!'

Her soft voice broke into his erotic thoughts and he knew that he must take control before he did something unforgivable—like kiss her.

'Yes?' he snapped.

How moody he could be, Sorrel thought. And

what a timely reminder that it might hurt a bit—sometimes more than others—but ultimately it was better to be out of his life and living her own on the other side of the world from him.

'We're here.'

The limo had drawn up outside a hotel and it was as Sorrel had predicted—for the sign outside read Etoile de la Mer.

'Bravo, Sorrel!' he applauded softly.

As the name suggested, the Etoile de la Mer was situated overlooking the sea—the kind of venue which played host to visiting politicians and stars who performed at the local theatres. A minor member of the British royal family had been conducting an extra-marital affair for many years within its luxurious walls. It was discreet, luxurious, and very expensive.

Outside, it was unremarkable only in its quiet restraint. Two perfectly clipped bay trees stood sentry, and several burly-looking doorman with calculating eyes stood beside the revolving door, ready to keep the unwanted away.

Inside, however, it was apparent why the Etoile de la Mer had achieved a small fame of its own. The view from the restaurant itself was simply breathtaking—a stunning sweep of the English Channel, whose watery-smooth surface reflected the moonlight.

Malik's people had obviously been hard at work before their arrival, and Sorrel knew that the intention would have been to ensure the maximum security with the least fuss. Few inside the restaurant would realise who had just walked in—until after the Sheikh had been ushered to the best, most carefully shielded table in the room.

Even if they *were* noticed it was doubtful whether they would be disturbed. Restaurants like this counted on their clientele being well-connected and famous enough to be diplomatic about their fellow-guests—certainly not crass enough to slip out to the restroom to telephone the gossip column of one of the national newspapers and announce that

Sheikh Malik of Kharastan was dining alone with a blonde!

Waiting to greet them was Rafiq—one of Malik's closest aides and a man known to Sorrel since childhood, for he had often advised her father on Kharastani policy. He must now be in his late forties, she decided—but her instinctively friendly smile of greeting froze in her face when it was met with a perfunctory cool nod from the learned Kharastani advisor.

'How are you, Sorrel?' he enquired with heavy formality, as if he had met her only minutes before.

'I am well, thank you,' she returned faintly.

'If you will allow me to show you to your table, Highness?' said Rafiq in soft, rapid Kharastani—presumably so that he would not be understood by the Maître d', who had just materialised by his side with a look of barely restrained excitement. 'I have organised everything to your pleasure.'

They moved towards their table, and unexpectedly Sorrel blinked in surprise as she caught sight of herself in one of the mirrors which reflected the sea back into the room. Her rose-pink T-shirt and flouncy gipsy skirt were just about presentable enough for a place like this—though they certainly did not carry the expected price-tag for a royal dining companion—but it was her expression which momentarily startled her. The way her eyes looked like giant blue saucers in the pale-gold of her face and her lips formed a rather anxious-looking 'O' shape.

Was that because she was nervous of Malik and what he was about to say to her—or because she had never been more glaringly aware of how tall and dynamic he looked? How the fluid cut of his very Western suit seemed to emphasise his dark beauty, the dark olive of his skin and the sensual promise of his hard, muscular body.

Two waiters appeared as if by clockwork to pull their chairs back, and menus were brought, dealt with and dispatched again—the wine list imperiously waved away and the waiter hurriedly sent to bring back a selection of soft drinks for the Sheikh to choose from.

Fariq, too, had melted away, and Sorrel folded her hands in her lap, like an obedient child—though in her case it was to prevent Malik from seeing how much they were trembling. And no wonder. It wasn't easy, sitting opposite him like this and trying not to drink in the pleasure of looking at the high, angled slant of his cheekbones and the lush black lashes which shielded the glitter of his eyes. Her heart was pounding as if she had been running in a race, and she knew that she had to pull herself together.

'So, Malik?' she said slowly.

For a moment he said nothing. He had learned to bide his time. To wait for the precise moment to strike. Just as the falcon did when it floated seamlessly on a warm current of desert air…circling, circling…until its prey was foolishly lulled into believing that it was safe.

And then it pounced.

He studied her face dispassionately. Her lips were parted, so that he could just make out the moist gleam of her tongue through tiny white teeth, and he found himself having to swallow down a sudden thickness which was threatening to constrict his throat.

And suddenly it was not so easy to think strategy. To think like the falcon. He was thinking like a man, and it was not appropriate—not with Sorrel. For the first time since he had conceived the idea he began to question it. And yet what was he, if not a man of strength and resolve? If he was sexually frustrated then he would take a temporary lover—and it would not be the flaxen-haired innocent who sat before him so expectantly.

'Do you ever miss Kharastan?' he asked.

Sorrel hesitated, but she knew that she had to answer this one truthfully—because anything else would be a betrayal of all the love and affection she had for his home. 'Yes,

I miss it,' she said quietly. 'I feel like there is an empty space in my heart sometimes.'

He suppressed his sigh of triumph. 'And you enjoy your job here in Brighton?' he queried with a careless air, as if it didn't matter, but Sorrel knew that Malik never wasted words.

'It's okay,' she said truthfully. 'Very different to what I was doing at the palace, of course!'

'So I understand,' he said coldly. 'It seems that you cater for the needs of backpackers.' He bit the last word out as if it were poison.

Sorrel felt that she ought to stand up for the great majority who didn't live in palaces. 'We have a varied clientele,' she said primly, 'who just want to see a different side of things.'

'It is not the kind of job which has any future,' he accused.

She considered this—knowing that it was pointless saying something she didn't mean, because the razor-tongued Malik would slice through her argument like a knife through a ripe melon. 'Not long-term, no,' she admitted.

He lifted his glass to his lips and sipped some soda, and then put it back down again, his eyes never leaving her face. 'I don't want you working there any more,' he stated flatly. 'I want you to accompany me on my European tour instead.'

Her heart was pounding beneath her breast, but bizarrely Sorrel's initial reaction to Malik's suggestion was indignation that he had said it in the tone of someone who was marshalling his troops. I *want*, he had said. An order, not a request. She guessed there was a difference between *want* and *like*, but Malik had never had to worry about the most diplomatic way of asking for something. What Malik wanted, Malik got.

Playing for time, she stared at him. 'And why on earth should you want me to do that?'

He thought he must have misheard her. 'Why?' he echoed. 'You dare to ask me *why*?'

'That's right.'

Malik frowned. He was used to acquiescence. Subservience. She had already got her way over this ridiculous request to find independence in England—and even though he had been forced to rescue her from that disreputable crowd it seemed that she had still not learnt her lesson. While sometimes he might think to himself that it was tedious never to be challenged—he now realised that he might have been mistaken. When would she learn that he was *always* right?

'Is it not enough that your Sheikh commands it?' he queried softly.

For a moment she didn't respond—because, despite his unashamedly autocratic tone, Sorrel was woman enough to thrill to that masterful entreaty. Yet it's *wrong* to react like that to his arrogance, she reminded herself. You know it is.

'Not really, Malik. No.'

For a moment he thought that she was joking—why else would she even hesitate over the opportunity he was offering her?

'You mean you are turning down my offer?' he demanded, outraged that she should even try.

For the first time since they'd walked in Sorrel smiled—for this was Malik at his predictable best. How black and white he always made everything seem! But wasn't that always the way of Kharastani men, and of the ruling class in particular? This went some way towards explaining why Fariq had behaved so frostily towards her—she doubted that he approved of Malik's wish to have her by his side.

'Do you consider me an intelligent woman?' she mused.

'Intelligent?' His eyes glittered as they surveyed her. 'You were not showing much evidence of it in your apartment earlier, with that bunch of—' His lips curled in derision. *'Drunks.'*

'Is that a yes or a no, Malik?'

Malik stared at her cool blue eyes. She had taken a First in Middle-Eastern studies at Kumush Ay University, and had been offered a research post there—nobody could deny that she had a brain and that she could use it. But having a brain was different from having common sense. 'Yes,' he admitted grudgingly—although he could not see what bearing this had on his original request.

'*Thank* you,' she said sarcastically. 'Just as I think of you as an intelligent man.'

'Why, thank *you*!' he returned, and for the first time in a long time Malik realised that he was enjoying himself—he was impatient for the waiter to deposit the plates of fine seafood and the raspberry cocktails on the table, so that he could continue with this verbal sparring which was so rare for a man in his position.

'So if I were ever to offer you some kind of position in *my* life, as an intelligent man I would expect you to ask me all kinds of questions about it before you agreed to take it.'

Malik stared at her in amazement. 'All that to make a point, Sorrel?' he queried faintly.

Sorrel shook her head. 'All that to try and

make you see *my* point of view,' she corrected. 'So, will you please tell me what it is you want of me?'

For one moment he very nearly told her—until he pulled himself together, reminding himself that it was the frisson of their disagreement which had renewed this terrible sexual aching. Malik found himself glaring at her, as if she had aroused him deliberately. Did he still want her help? he wondered. Was it worth risking?

But then his mind leapt ahead as he envisaged the whistlestop tour his advisors had worked out for him, and he knew that, yes, it was.

He inclined his dark head slightly. 'I want you behind the scenes, helping me—just as you used to help my father, the Sheikh.'

'But you have proper advisors to do that,' objected Sorrel.

How could he begin to explain that the formal and older Fariq and his younger but equally formal assistants were like robots? That the thought of major cities—even Paris, which he had once visited as an impressionable boy on the cusp of manhood—no longer held any allure for him. Not now. It would be all signing papers and starchy meetings. Although surrounded by hordes of people eager to accede to his every whim, he would be alone in the truest sense of the word.

'Yes,' he said, more heavily than he had intended to—and then his black eyes narrowed slightly, as if he had shown her an unexpected chink in his defences that she might store up to use against him. But Sorrel was not a manipulator—she did not have enough experience of the world to have learnt *how* to manipulate—and wasn't that one of the reasons he wanted her with him? 'I am not expecting you to suddenly take on the role of political advisor,' he said testily.

'Well, what *would* my role be?'

Malik thought about it. 'As a kind of social companion,' he said carefully.

'Which sounds like the kind of post you

might offer to a woman over fifty!' Sorrel stared at him. 'Would you mind elaborating, please?'

He tried and failed to think of another woman—or man, even—he would allow to get away with speaking to him in such a manner. 'I will have functions to attend. Long dinners. Cocktails. Afternoons at the races. Visits to museums. War memorials. It would lessen the burden considerably if I had someone I knew well to accompany me. Someone with whom I can discuss and assess afterwards.' He opened his eyes a fraction wider, like a cat which had just been awoken from a long sleep. 'Someone who can stop people from getting too close to me. Especially women.'

Sorrel ignored the implied boast, even though she felt a sudden stab of jealousy. 'A kind of gatekeeper, you mean?' she questioned coolly.

'Precisely.'

'Fariq could do that just as well.'

'Fariq isn't quite so easy on the eye.'

For a moment Sorrel didn't quite believe that

she'd heard him properly. Malik, saying that she was *attractive*? She stared at him suspiciously. 'And what's that supposed to mean?'

Malik lowered his voice, even though they had both been speaking in Kharastani. 'Oh, come, come, Sorrel,' he murmured, mock-reprovingly. 'Don't be disingenuous—for it scorns the intelligence you hold so dear! Flaxen hair and blue eyes on a pretty and shapely young woman are the hallmarks of beauty, as well you know.'

Defiantly, she speared a seared scallop and ate it—partly to defuse her annoyance at his remarks and partly to give her time to answer a compliment which he had managed to make sound like an insult! Disingenuous, indeed! What did Malik know?

She might tick all the right boxes in attributes that men seemed to want—but the outside stuff had nothing to do with what was going on *inside*. And inside she was as mixed-up and as wobbly on self-esteem as the next woman.

She'd had no real boyfriend. No lover to reassure her that she was gorgeous—though maybe she shouldn't be relying on a *man* to booster her feelings of self-worth. Maybe she should dig deep and find them within herself.

'So you want some arm-candy?' she questioned flippantly.

Malik scowled. 'Such a short time in England and already you are conversant with slang!' he accused.

'It's all part of my education to enter the modern world, Malik. I can't go on living in an ivory tower for ever.'

'And just how *comprehensive* an education are you seeking?' he enquired dangerously.

'Who knows?' She saw his eyes darken with rage, and with something else she didn't recognise—and suddenly Sorrel felt empowered by her own sense of freedom. 'That's my business,' she answered softly, and the words hung and shimmered on the air like morning dewdrops on the web of a spider.

'Mine also,' he said, and his words were equally soft.

Their eyes met—hers questioning the grim certainty in his.

'You think so?' she questioned.

'I know so! I cannot abandon a lifetime's habit and wash my hands of you as if you no longer exist,' he grated.

'Is that why you're offering me the post?' she demanded. 'So that you can keep your eye on me.'

'I can assure you that my motives are far more selfish than that, Sorrel.' He leaned forward just a little—so that she could see the black glitter of his eyes, as dark and as hard as jet itself. 'You could prove very useful to me on this trip—for you *know me* better than anyone.'

Once she would have agreed with him. He had not known the identity of his father until just before he died, and his mother had slipped away in childbirth—so, yes, during her growing up Sorrel had been close to him. But that had been before he had inherited the Kharastani crown—an event which now seemed so long ago that it was like a lifetime.

Yet it was only two years, she realised with a start. Sorrel bit her lip as an immense wave of sadness washed over her—hating the inevitable changes which time had wrought.

What had he just said—that she could prove very *useful* to him? What a damning testimony *that* was. A bullet-proof car was *useful*, and so was soft pillow on which to place your weary head at night—but Sorrel would have hoped to have had a more flattering word than that applied to her. And that was where the trouble lay—she was a fool where Malik was concerned. Deep down she hankered after much more than he would ever be prepared to give her.

If took him up on his request—went with him to all his glamorous destinations—then wouldn't she just get sucked into his life once more? Only next time find it even harder to grab the courage to say goodbye?

'I notice that still you make me wait for your answer,' Malik observed slowly, but his eyes gleamed with the anticipation of a certain victory.

Grabbing all the pluck she possessed, Sorrel met the soft dark blaze of his eyes and steeled herself against its hypnotic beauty. 'I can't do it, Malik,' she whispered.

'Can't? Or won't?'

'Doesn't it amount to the same thing?'

A muscle began to work in his cheek. 'Would you mind telling me why?'

And Sorrel suddenly realised that she was going to have to come up with something about which there could be no argument—something he couldn't try to talk her out of. Something *true*—but something shocking. So that the Sheikh would regret ever having asked her. But she recognised as she opened her mouth to say the words that they would change his opinion of her—and damn her for ever in his fierce and puritanical eyes.

'Because I need a lover, Malik,' she said huskily. 'That's why.'

CHAPTER FIVE

FOR A MOMENT, Malik could not quite believe what he had heard—and he stared at her for a long and disbelieving moment. Sorrel—his sometimes feisty but always innocent ward—had just announced that she wanted a lover! Which was as inconceivable as the morning sun rising a sickly shade of green instead of its habitual gold.

'*What* did you say?' he questioned unevenly.

Never had Sorrel heard the Sheikh's voice sound so dangerous, so forbidding, so...*scary*. But she told herself that she was an adult—free to do as she wished—and she did not have to answer to *him*! Nevertheless, she backed away from actually repeating the words to the formidable presence who was seated opposite her, simmering with a quiet dark rage.

'You know what I said.'

'That you want a *lover*!' he sneered. 'How can this be?'

They were speaking in Kharastani, and their voices were so low that even the bodyguards seated a discreet distance away would not have heard what they were saying—but the venom in Malik's accusation must have carried across the room, because several of the well-heeled diners jerked their heads up and frowned, before tactfully returning their attention to their meals.

The accusation which burned angrily from his ebony eyes washed over her in a black fire, but Sorrel knew that she could not allow him to psychologically defeat her. She was a woman, for heaven's sake—not some little doll which was dressed up and brought out on state occasions. 'What's wrong with that?' she said, more airily than she felt inside.

'Wrong? *Wrong*?' Rarely had Malik remembered feeling such a raw and blinding rage. He wanted to lash out. He wanted…

His long olive fingers briefly flexed, made an even briefer claw-like shape, before clenching into tight and angry fists on the starched white linen tablecloth. Could it really be *Sorrel* who was saying this? Sorrel—his ward—the young ward he had watched over like a hawk. Sweet, flaxen-haired Sorrel, who'd used to run around the palace gardens—indulged by all who came across her sunny smile. Sorrel the innocent… the…

Or was that an assumption too far? Like the ones he had stupidly made about her unquestioning obedience and her loyalty to him as her Sheikh? Did her desire for a man to know her in such a way mean that she had already tasted the fruits of intimacy? Enjoyed the pleasures of the flesh in a way which had made her hungry for more? A shaft of something which felt like pain but which he put down to outrage caught him by the throat. She had denied it once, but that did not mean she had spoken the truth!

'You are no longer a virgin?' he demanded hoarsely.

Sorrel felt the stain of a blush flare up from the base of her throat to burn in tell-tale spots upon her cheeks. How bizarre that he felt he had the right to ask her something as intimately personal as this *in a restaurant*!

But didn't you ask for it? mocked a small voice in her head. *By stating your crass desire to find yourself a lover?*

Reminding herself that she *did* want to live like any other young woman, she stared at him.

'You've already asked me that, Malik.'

'And I am giving you the opportunity to retract your statement.'

'We are *not* in a court of law!' she stormed.

He ignored that, leaning across the table towards her. 'Do you speak the truth, Sorrel?' His black eyes bored into her. 'Are you still a virgin?'

Their eyes did furious battle—until Sorrel realised that it was a pointless one. What was the point of pretending an experience that was sadly lacking if it would damn her even further in his opinion?

'Yes,' she admitted. 'I am. And the one thing I am *not* is a liar, Malik!'

He was unprepared for the flame of triumph which blazed through him, surging in a heated stream through his veins, but he did not show it, merely sucked a still-angry breath in through his nostrils—like his most temperamental stallion when he was thwarted. He must, he realised, play this very carefully—for Sorrel was *not* being obedient. Far from it. But she would be made to bend to his will, without even comprehending that she was doing so! He uttered a silent prayer of thanks, without understanding why it should be so important to him. Because it meant he would have failed in his role as her guardian?

'So why the urge to change that state?' he

questioned, in a cool voice which was a million miles away from the inner turmoil of his feelings. But he was good at disguising his feelings—as a child it had been a necessity, and as aide to the Sheikh he had quickly learned that it was inappropriate to *have* feelings. And hadn't that been the most invaluable training for his new position? 'It sounds rather an *impetuous* decision,' he drawled.

How cold his eyes. And how disapproving his demeanour, which had the power to make her feel like a gauche young girl—or maybe that was his intention? Suddenly Sorrel wanted him to hear the truth, not a sanitised version of it told to protect the precious royal ears.

'Because….because I'm twenty-five years old and I feel like I've spent the whole of my live in a convent!'

'You mean you have been protected from the carnal desires of men?' he elaborated savagely.

Sorrel licked her lips nervously. Had she been expecting such an angry response? The answer was that she hadn't really thought it through properly.

'I mean that I want to live like other women of my age!' she declared. 'Or rather I want to *live*! I'm fed-up with conforming to other people's standards. I want to be able to show my legs without feeling that I'm breaking some kind of moral code, to dance late at night and drink alcohol, and…and…'

'And have sex?'

Why the hell was he making something which was perfectly healthy and normal sound so fundamentally wrong?

'What's wrong with that?' She sighed. 'Other women my age do.'

'Other women your age are not *you*.'

Sorrel shook her head in frustration. 'And just what is that, Malik—huh? Who *am* I? Someone who is like a stranger in her own country and yet can never fit into her adopted country.'

'Why not?' he questioned coolly.

'Because…because….' *Because I adore you*

and there can never be any future with you—and that's even if you had ever bothered to look at me as a woman rather than as someone who just fits in with your unrealistic wishes.
'Because I can never have true independence in Kharastan.'

'And that is what you want? That is what matters to you? To wear the revealing clothes and have the sex?'

She had never heard him sound so... *foreign*... But then she had never seen him so het up before. And the truth was that these things were not really what she wanted—but what they represented. If she had carried on living in Kharastan then she would have spent all her youth and her life living in the shadow of a man who would one day marry another. And Sorrel knew that she couldn't have stood there and watched it happen.

Malik was so egotistical that it wouldn't even occur to him that it might hurt. Why, she could even imagine him thoughtlessly requesting that she help his new wife settle in—maybe even help with any progeny they might produce. And she couldn't do that—she really couldn't. It would rip her heart in two if she ever had to deal with Malik's beautiful black-eyed children by another woman.

'Maybe these things *do* matter,' Sorrel said, expecting another furious tirade—but to her surprise there was none. Just that narrow-eyed and considering look from those glitteringly intelligent eyes which those who knew Malik had learned to be wary of.

'And you think that if you accompanied me on my tour I would prevent you from doing these things?' he questioned.

Was he *kidding*? Or was it just one of Malik's devilishly clever plans which had made him one of his region's most feared and respected rulers in just two short years? Sorrel decided to call his bluff. 'Are you really implying that you'd give me your blessing to start living a liberal life if I decided to join you?'

For the first time he partook of a little food—crumbling a bread roll between his fingers and eating a piece of it thoughtfully rather than eagerly. He ate little, Sorrel realised—he always had—and she guessed that explained why his body was harder and leaner than those of other men. It was like the difference between a pampered domestic cat and a predator that existed on its wits in the forest. He picked up his water glass and drank from it, so that when he put the glass down and lifted his gaze to hers his lips gleamed, as did his black eyes.

'That depends.'

Sorrel blinked, putting down her fork, which still speared a half-gnawed piece of fish—because this whole situation was so bizarre that she had completely lost what little appetite she'd had.

'Depends?' Her voice trembled as she looked at him, and so did her body. 'Depends on what?'

'On just who you elect to be the lucky recipient of your sexual favours.'

'Malik, you make it sound so…'

'Vulgar?'

'Well, yes.'

He shrugged. 'I agree entirely. But surely you have only yourself to blame? You did not express a wish for the hearts and the flowers that I assumed all young women yearned for when they lost their maidenhood—you simply made it sound like a mechanical act.'

Now he was humiliating her. 'I don't want to talk about it any more!' she vowed fiercely. 'Let's just forget it.'

Malik shook his dark head in a resolute and decisive movement that Sorrel had seen many times before.

'I cannot forget it,' he said simply. No indeed—for now he was haunted by vivid and graphic and infinitely disturbing images of her pale, bare body tangled with that of a man. Being penetrated by another…her beautiful, sunny and innocent face crying out first her pain and then her pleasure. Her long, shapely legs—which he had only seen for the first time himself tonight—wrapped around the back of an interloper. Someone else who would fill her with his seed… He winced, halfway himself between pain and pleasure, and having to suppress a small sound of protest. 'But I have a solution which I think might suit us both.'

Sorrel's senses prickled with alarm, and with something else, too—something she wasn't really sure she recognised. 'I'm not with you.'

He smiled, but it was a calculating, almost cruel smile. 'You want a lover?' he said softly. 'Well, so do I. You want to learn the delights of lovemaking? Then let me be your tutor—for you will find none better.'

Her heart was pounding fit to deafen her—but a thousand nebulous dreams exploded into a shivering feeling of fear as they became a possible reality. 'You mean…you…*you*… would…?'

With a grim kind of satisfaction he noted the rosy colour which had bloomed in her cheeks as he listened to her stumbled words. How naïve she was! How the hell was she expecting to cope in a world of sexual predators? he thought soberly. With her flaxen hair and her delicate blush she looked heart-stoppingly innocent. Why, he should throw her to the lions and let her discover for herself just how foolhardy she was being. But then he felt the hard weight of his erection pressing against his leg and knew that he could not bear for another man to touch her. Not before he did…

'Yes, I would be your tutor,' he agreed softly, drinking in the blue confusion of her widened eyes. 'Would that be so reprehensible a gesture?'

She was about to say yes, when he spoke about it like that—with all the lack of emotion he might employ if he were reading out a shopping list. Except that Malik would never have to even *look* at a shopping list, she reminded herself. 'I just hadn't…' But her words tailed off. She knew that he might detect the lie in them if she said she hadn't ever thought of him in terms of lover when she'd spent years fantasising about just that.

'Hadn't what, Sorrel?' he prompted throatily. 'Hadn't got around to picking a candidate? Well, then, you have the very best available.' His black eyes glittered with anticipation of pleasures to come. 'For every woman I have bedded has told me that I am the greatest lover of all,' he murmured, totally without shame.

It was stupid and illogical, but this *hurt*. *Really* hurt. Of course somewhere in the back of her mind Sorrel knew that he'd had lovers—and that there had probably been lots of them. Malik was certainly no innocent—he exuded an air of sexuality which was as natural to him as breathing. He was bred to be sensual in the same way that the falcon was bred to move in for the kill—but she had never heard it voiced before, and his boast made her picture him with other women. How many? she wondered jealously. How *many*?

He noted her hesitation and, oddly enough, it pleased him—for a man would take little joy in a prize easily won. 'What I am offering you is a scenario that most women would yearn for,' he mused, and traced the tip of his finger along the lush pad of his bottom lip, knowing that her eyes followed the movement and knowing perfectly well what effect it would have on her. 'You will be taken to the most glamorous places in the world and you will stay in the lap of luxury—and there you will be given the most comprehensive education possible in the art of seduction.'

It was a cold-blooded itinerary for something so significant, and Sorrel knew that she ought to say that it was a preposterous idea—but she was distracted by the erotic gesture of Malik stroking his mouth like that. Was he doing it deliberately? she wondered. Aware that her eyes would be mesmerised by the slow and tantalising gesture—that she would be imagining him stroking *her* lips like that…

But could she bear to have him as her lover? To give him her body when he had already captured her heart? Wouldn't that be a risk too far? Say no, urged the calm, inner voice of reason—but reason was vanquished by a sudden and unexpected source.

A svelte redhead was sitting on the other side of the restaurant, at a table which afforded a perfect view of Malik's hard and autocratic face.

Sorrel had noticed the woman staring over—but that was nothing new and she had paid her little attention. With his dark, slightly dangerous good-looks people were always staring at Malik.

But some transformation had occurred at his suggestion that he could fulfil the role of Sorrel's sensual tutor—and it felt awfully like *possession*. That he was *hers*—or rather he *could* be hers—and wasn't that almost as dangerous as the unrequited love she had felt for him for years? Because Malik could never be hers—not in any real sense. He was too proud and too cold to give himself to her emotionally, even if strict Kharastani custom meant that he could never marry a woman not of his own blood.

Marry him! Now, where the hell had *that* come from? Age seemed to have taught her nothing if she was having the kind of bizarre fantasy that she wouldn't even have been foolish enough to entertain at the age of sixteen!

Malik had been studying her with the kind of detached interest with which a scientist might peer into a test tube as he waited for her answer—but the new focus of her gaze in the direction of the redhead made him frown, and his eyes narrowed as he glanced over at the Titian-haired beauty.

The woman had clearly been to a colour expert who must have advised her that green was the way to go—her very womanly curves were squeezed into a luscious mint-green cocktail dress which provided a wonderful backdrop for the rich lustre of her hair. Her scarlet lips were pouting, and she didn't seem to be listening to a word that her dining partner was saying to her.

For one second—like an invisible observer—Sorrel watched the interplay between the stranger and the Sheikh. *I want you,* the woman's eyes said—as clearly as if she had shouted the words out at the top of her voice.

Sorrel sneaked a glance at Malik, who had allowed a small and rueful smile to play around the curved perfection of his mouth. Was she imagining it, or was his glittered look a silent acknowledgement, *I want you, too,* or was she just going crazy? Crazy or not, Sorrel felt a tug of an emotion so primitive and powerful that for a moment she couldn't breathe. She looked at the naked hunger on the beauty's face, and knew with certainty that *she* would have taken up Malik's offer without a moment's thought.

Malik had no need to pick up strange women in restaurants—no matter how stunning they were—but he had already said that he wanted a lover.

Sorrel bit her lip perplexedly. So, did she turn down his offer—make the wise decision and just walk away?

Or did she give in to her heart and body's desire and take what was so beautifully on offer—even if it risked the complete wreckage of all her dreams?

But maybe dreams had to be smashed to allow you to carry on living with some degree of contentment in the real world?

'Okay,' she said, shrugging her shoulders like an awkward schoolgirl and wishing that they were alone somewhere, so that the arrangement could have been sealed in the traditional way.

'*Okay?*' Malik frowned. It was not the jubilant acceptance which was his due, and clearly she had no idea of the great honour he was affording her. But she would soon learn, he thought grimly.

Sorrel shifted in her chair as practical considerations began to rear their heads. 'What will…? Well, what on earth is Fariq going to think about the arrangement?'

Malik gave a short laugh. 'I'm not exactly planning to go on national television to announce it.'

His sarcasm should maybe have warned her that she was playing with fire—and everyone knew what happened to people who did that—but it was too late to back out now, even if she'd wanted to. But if their sexual arrangement was to resemble some sort of business arrangement, then they really ought to establish ground-rules right at the beginning.

'You mean it's going to have to be a secret? Fariq won't know?'

'Of course he will *know*,' he said softly. 'But, as usual, he will turn a blind eye, and we will be discreet.'

His words made it perfectly clear that this was how these things worked. Smoke and mirrors and discretion. 'Of course.'

Her lips were trembling, and he found himself

swamped with an overpowering desire to kiss them. He turned towards the aide seated unobtrusively at another table and glimmered him a look—and the whole machinery for the Sheikh leaving a restaurant was set into motion.

He signalled for her to follow him out, but her hands were clammy with nerves as the small cluster of hotel management who were mingling with his staff moved forward to accompany them to the executive lift.

'Leave us now,' Malik ordered his bodyguards, once the door of the penthouse apartment had been opened, and Faliq, who had silently appeared from within, gave a short bow and followed them—though Sorrel knew she hadn't mistaken the faint look of shock and disapproval on his face.

Malik closed the door behind them, and put his hands on her shoulders.

'So, we are alone at last,' he murmured, and his voice was thick with desire. 'Your lesson must begin.'

She could feel his hands burning into her flesh through the T-shirt she wore, and suddenly Sorrel felt unprepared—unworthy of her sheikh lover.

'You mean…*now*?'

Her face was a mere hand's width away, and never before had he been so aware of the sapphire blueness of her eyes—as gleaming and as bright as the colour of his beloved Balsora sea on a hot summer day.

'Now?' he echoed huskily, not quite under-standing.

'You want us to go to bed now?'

Malik's mouth hardened, first with anger and then with a grim determination. She was wise to have adopted him as her tutor—but would he soon be regretting his swift folly in having offered himself?

'This, of course, is the trouble with modern women,' he said witheringly. 'They wish to devour the feast without tasting the food—like snacking straight from the fridge—and, pray tell me, where is the pleasure or the enjoyment in that?'

It sounded like a reprimand—indeed, it *was* a reprimand. Sorrel stared at him, hoping that she was hiding her hurt feelings, but she found herself blurting out words of reproach. 'You can't expect me to be an expert on these matters, Malik.'

'No.' Bizarrely, he found himself wanting to kiss her—even though she had not prepared herself for him. And despite his reservations, and his certainty that he should send her away to bathe, Malik gave in to his desire. 'Come,' he commanded, and pulled her into the warm circle of his arms, her handbag falling to the floor as her face turned automatically up to his, like a flower to the sun. 'Come let me kiss you,' he murmured, his lips driving down on hers with a raw hunger which was outside his experience.

She tasted of elderflowers and she smelled of lilacs and her trembling body sang of her purity—and Malik found himself trembling too, as her mouth opened beneath the seeking insistence of his.

'Oh, Malik!' she breathed, her arms flying up uninhibitedly to his neck, coiling around him as you sometimes saw a sleeping snake coiled around the charmers in the heat-dazed market square of Kumush Ay.

She pressed her body eagerly against his, so that her soft pliancy was moulded against the hard contours of his, and Malik could scarcely breathe—for he was taken aback by the openness with which she offered herself. For one split second he imagined her honeyed warmth and tightness, and the hardness of his body felt too close to torture to be bearable.

He could take her here and now. Kiss her into an easy submission and lay her down on the carpet. Why, he would not even need to undress her—because none of his aides would dare enter until he gave them permission. He could push up that filmy gipsy skirt and rip off her panties and…and…

'Malik!' she breathed once more.

He gave a little moan and pushed her away from him, glaring as he released her. 'What did I just tell you?' he demanded.

Dazedly, Sorrel stared at him. Now what? She'd thought he'd been enjoying the kiss as much as she was. 'Did I...did I do something wrong?'

'Yes! No!' He shook his head in frustration. 'These are supposed to be exercises in sensual restraint—a slow build-up to eventual delights—not that...that *frenzied* demonstration.' A demonstration which made his own lovemaking boasts sound distinctly hollow. The best lover of all? Why, he had responded like an eager schoolboy!

Abruptly, Malik turned away and stalked down the corridor towards the vast salon. Sorrel stared after his angry back for a moment, before deciding that there wasn't a lot of choice other than to follow him.

Lost in thought, he stood staring out of the

window, at the dancing sea which was coloured inky and indigo by the night, except where moonlight topped the waves with little slicks of silver. He heard the sound of her footsteps, and he steeled himself to demonstrate the fine balance between control and need which would be necessary for him to conduct this somewhat unconventional liaison.

Arrangements must be put into place—and quickly—because they would be leaving for Madrid almost immediately.

'There are many preparations which need to be made,' he said softly. 'But not tonight. Tonight you need to go to bed.' Reaching out, he traced the pad of his thumb over the shadows beneath her eyes, meeting the startled look which darkened her blue eyes and shaking his head in answer to her unspoken question. 'Alone.'

A hurt look which she managed to twist into a wry smile curved Sorrel's lips as she left to retrieve her handbag. She very nearly said *So what else is new?* For hadn't she spent the whole of her life alone?

CHAPTER SIX

THE NEXT morning, Sorrel wondered if she had dreamt it all. Malik gate-crashing her party and then whisking her away from it and telling her that he would teach her everything she needed to know about love. But then she touched a finger to her kiss-bruised lips and knew it had all been real.

She'd woken with the scent of the Sheikh on her skin—tasting him on her lips—and she shivered as she showered herself with a brand-new self-awareness. As she pulled on her underwear and fished out the one long silk Kharastani tunic she'd brought to England with her she wondered if she was doing the right thing.

But who could she possibly ask?

There was no one. She was—and always had been—a lone agent. Even when her parents had been alive she had felt very much in the background. They had loved her as best they could—but had been consumed by their passion for foreign culture and the adventure of exploring inaccessible terrain.

She looked around the rented flat. In a neat pile on the desk was her passport and a few papers. Her clothes filled two suitcases, and a bag of rubbish containing a few yoghurts and some mouldy fruit was waiting to be dumped in the bin outside. Not much to show for her new-found and independent life, was it? And any minute now...

The doorbell trilled and Sorrel went to open it. Another aide, most probably.

But it was not an aide. It was Malik himself. And it was Malik looking like the man she knew—dark, elemental man of the desert, more at home on horseback or holding out one iron-hard arm to greet the re-turning falcon.

Gone was the immaculate Western suit he had been wearing yesterday—today he was in traditional Kharastani attire. A flowing tunic, made from the very finest silk, which shim-mered as he moved and hinted at the hard body beneath. He looked as out of place on the doorstep of this very English building as a bird of paradise would appear if it landed in the centre of a city square.

'Malik,' she breathed.

'I see that you are dressed more appropriately today,' he murmured—and yet wasn't it typical of human nature that you always wanted what you hadn't got? Yesterday, he had been outraged to see those long, slender thighs on display, and yet today, when they were demurely covered, he found himself missing them.

Sorrel smoothed a rueful hand down over the flat of her hip. 'It's the only one I've brought with me. It's very old.'

'Yes. I can see that.' He frowned. 'But you had the services of the palace dressmaker—why did you not use her more?'

Sorrel met the narrowed black eyes. 'I did not feel it was appropriate.'

'Why not?'

Would it sound pathetic if she told him that she hadn't felt comfortable about dressing up for palace events? 'I was there as a functionary, Malik. To blend into the background, rather than stand out from it.'

Such an unassuming point of view had simply never occurred to him—even before he had acceded to the throne. Other than his lovers—all of whom would have had the dressmaker working for them non-stop—Malik had known few women. His mother had died in childbirth and he had been fussed over by the palace servants, but there had not been any one continuous role-model figure. If he had been asked to select the woman he had been closest to he would have plumped for

Sorrel—but now it seemed that he did not know her at all. Did that go some way towards explaining her sudden transformation in England? A woman who had paid very little attention to fashion suddenly being thrown in at the deep end of modern culture?

Malik scowled. Why was he wasting his time worrying about it?

'Whilst your modesty is admirable, you will need a new wardrobe for the trip. You will be in effect, a kind of female ambassador for Kharastan.'

'I *will*?'

He nodded. 'For too long our international standing has been open to criticism. The view has been that our women are oppressed—and one of your tasks will be to demonstrate otherwise.'

'You're rather supposing that I don't go along with that view myself?'

Black eyes bored into her. 'And do you?'

Sorrel shook her head and sighed. How

much easier it would be if she did. But, in a way, she could see that women had room to flourish in a culture such as Kharastan. It was true that you couldn't go around wearing a mini-skirt—but Sorrel had witnessed for herself just how much trouble that could get you into. It didn't matter if you went around declaring that women had the right to show their legs—men were programmed to react in a certain way if you did!

'No, I don't,' she said. 'Although I'm not saying that Kharastani society is perfect—'

'No society is,' he put in, a small smile curving the corners of his mouth—until he remembered that there were three cars sitting outside waiting and that Fariq would be glowering in the way he'd been doing ever since Malik had expressed the desire to have Sorrel on the trip. 'But we are wasting time.'

He had taken a step towards her, and in the cold, bright light of the morning Sorrel was suddenly fearful of his dark look of sexual stealth. She took a step back. What the hell had she allowed herself to be talked into?

'You…you mean…I've got to go shopping?'

His hand reached out to capture her tiny waist and he snaked her towards him. 'Shopping?' he laughed softly. 'I think not—or do you imagine that the streets of Brighton could supply the best that Kharastan has to offer? No, Sorrel—you must not worry about clothes.'

Rubbing his finger reflectively at her waist, he thought that a body like hers worked best with no clothes at all. But would that not be part of the thrill for him—to have a woman he was forced to *wait* for? To anticipate, rather than have something offered to him as easily as breathing. He felt her shiver beneath his touch, and he smiled. 'I have already ordered what I want you to wear.'

Pleased to have something to distract herself from the tantalising promise of his touch, Sorrel stared up at him. 'How can you have?'

'The royal dressmaker has drawn you up a traditional wardrobe, but with a modern twist.'

'I still don't understand, Malik.'

'Well, the dressmaker knows your size—she has your measurements on file.' Black eyes roved with slow and almost insolent approval over her slender body. 'And you do not look to me as if you have gained any weight.' He frowned. 'Maybe lost just a little. I can see that I shall have to feed you, Sorrel—for we Kharastani men like our women to have some shape to them.'

Sorrel shook her head impatiently. He was being *deliberately* obtuse. 'The clothes are ready now?' And, when he nodded his affirmation, 'How *can* they be ready, when I only agreed to accompany you late last evening?'

'Because I made up my mind that I wanted you several weeks ago.'

Her heart flared with a hope which rapidly became pain as she reminded herself that he was talking practically, not sentimentally. 'But what if I hadn't…agreed?' she said slowly.

He shrugged his broad shoulders and didn't attempt to hide the arrogant complacency of his smile. 'I knew you would agree,' he said. 'You see, I always get what I want.'

Sorrel felt the alarming missed beat of her heart—anger that he had so cleverly manipulated her, but also that he appeared to show no regret for having done so.

'And what would you do if I told you that I have a will of my own?' she demanded heatedly. 'That despite the agreement made last night I have changed my mind? What if I told you that I intend to walk out right now? What would you do then?'

'Why, this,' he murmured hungrily. 'I would do this.' And he lowered his mouth to hers.

She wanted to fight it—she tried to fight it— her fists hammering redundantly at the muscular wall of his chest as she turned her head away from the hot and tempting brush of his mouth. Spurred on by his teasing little laugh, she tried to wriggle away. But the

movement became something else entirely—
bringing her into contact with the unmistakable
hardness in the very cradle of his groin.

Her eyes widened into saucers, like an old-
fashioned doll her mother had given her as a
child, and she turned once more and met the
mockery in his.

'Yes, Sorrel,' he said softly, watching the
slow realisation dawning on her face. 'You can
feel me. Feel how hard I am for you. How I
could now—were I to wish it—take you in the
most fundamental way possible.' He saw the
flare of colour which darkened her cheekbones. 'But that is not my intention. This will
be a slow and wonderful awakening—and
while we may have disagreements along the
way none of those will impact on your sensual
education. Come, kiss me.'

Their lips were now so close that she could
feel the warmth of his breath. Such a short
distance—but psychologically it was a huge
leap into the unknown. Sorrel knew that he

spoke the truth—that he always got what he wanted. Yet she also knew that Malik might be an autocratic ruler, who governed a distinctly male-dominated society, but even he would not have dragged her back and kept her prisoner if she really *had* wanted to walk out.

If she'd wanted to walk out…

How could she possibly do that? She had crossed some invisible line and there was no going back.

'Kiss me, Sorrel,' he urged, and for the first time a note of unashamed yearning darkened his voice.

'Oh, Malik.' Instinctively she held the moment, and then gave in to it, sinking against him as if in slow motion—the soft sweet temptation of his lips contrasting with the hardness of his body and the overpowering sense of having sealed her fate.

His lips teased hers open, with the tip of his tongue lightly flicking to and fro and setting alight the flicker of desire. She could feel it building as he continued to tease her, while his hands tangled luxuriantly in her hair, using it to draw her towards him, closer into the apex of his body.

It was as if he was orchestrating her movements by using some powerful and unseen force. How else did she seem to know what was required of her? Was that stifled little cry of hunger hers? And why were her hips circling against his like that, so that he groaned in response? She wondered if he could read her mind—because how else did he pick up her silent plea of protest that he deepen the kiss? Yet she felt torn when his tongue entered her mouth—because one answered prayer quickly became another, and she wanted more. Oh, much more.

'By the desert storm!' he ground out.

He let her go. Abruptly. A fast-shuttering movement of his eyes the only outward sign that he was disturbed. For a moment he did not move nor speak; he did not dare. One word or one touch and he would forget everything he had told her about restraint and waiting and lessons and demonstrations of his finesse. He wanted her as no other!

Because she is pure, he reasoned—not the glossy breed of woman you usually gravitate towards because they always give you what you want, with no questions asked and no demands made.

Sorrel opened her eyes, aware that her breathing was laboured and so was his. His eyes glittered as if he had a fever, and his skin was flushed beneath the olive glow. For a split-second she read the desire which fired out from beneath the heavily hooded black eyes— but in a moment it was gone, and in its place the habitual watchfulness which made people around him so wary.

'What is it?' she asked, wanting the passion back again. 'Why have you stopped?'

'You are an eager pupil,' he declared unsteadily.

For the first time she began to realise that maybe she'd made the most stupid bargain of all time. By agreeing to be tutored by Malik wasn't she in danger of consigning herself to a life where every other man would just fall into the imposing shadow of the Sheikh? For how could anyone else ever come close to making her feel the way he had just done in his arms?

'And you are an expert teacher,' she said.

He ran his eyes over her critically, knowing that the dreamy expression which still softened her flushed features was not fitting—not in these particular circumstances. She must learn that his position meant that different rules had to be in place—that she must be prepared to snap back to normality at a second's notice. To walk out to the waiting limousine as if they had been doing nothing more blameless than talking about their schedule.

'Go and wash your face and brush your hair,' he instructed, more roughly than he had intended, and to his consternation he saw her wince in response and lower her eyelashes to hide her pain. But didn't she realise that the smoky, come-hither look in her eyes was making him ache so badly that he wanted to just send the car away? To take her to bed as if they were just a normal man and woman who were allowing themselves the pleasures of the flesh?

Of course she doesn't realise, he told himself sternly. For she was innocent not only of men, but of the power of her own allure—and he must teach her how to channel it.

He touched a finger to her chin. 'Sorrel?' he said, in a voice which for him was almost gentle. 'Look at me.'

She blinked away the hint of rogue tears as she lifted her head to meet his gaze, wondering what she had done wrong—what had made him speak to her in that rough, impatient way. 'I do not please you,' she said dully.

In that one moment he wanted to forget the whole deal. He did not want to make her doubt herself. He wanted back the Sorrel that he knew—the intelligent and spirited woman he had watched grow into a beauty. But he had made the deal now, and she had bewitched him into wanting her—he would never be satisfied until he had known her intimately. Maybe making love to her would obliterate the relationship they had known—but that was a risk he had to take.

'You please me more than you could imagine,' he said softly. 'But I cannot just submit to desire when it takes me. I have a duty to fulfill and an image to maintain. And I must keep up my guard and my composure around the team who work for me. Sex weakens a man, Sorrel, and I cannot allow myself to be perceived as weak—not in any way. And that is why you must learn to switch your passion on and off.'

'As suits you?'

He shook his dark head. 'As suits us both. For—just as I need always to appear invulnerable—you too need protection. If we make it apparent that you are mistress to the Sheikh then we give my enemies ammunition with which to wound me.'

'You have enemies, Malik?' she questioned in a small voice, and the spear of pain she felt was pain for *him*.

How naïve she was! 'A ruler always has enemies.' He laughed, but it was an odd, humourless sort of laugh. 'Especially one who has had such an unusual transition into the job as I have. Now, do not look so worried, little one—or I shall not be able to concentrate on my job. Go and make yourself calm, and then we shall face Faliq. We have a plane fuelled and ready, and a deputation of dignitaries waiting in Madrid.'

She smiled at him and turned away, her heart lifting as she walked towards the bathroom. *He hasn't called me 'little one' in years.* But she banished the rogue thought, reminding herself that he had made it clear from the start that this was a practical and not an emotional relationship.

So start acting that way, she told herself, as she splashed cold water onto her heated cheeks and brushed her mussed hair.

Next stop Spain, she thought, peering one last time at her reflection in the mirror.

And then she walked out to meet the waiting Sheikh.

CHAPTER SEVEN

'WILL you be wanting me for anything else, Highness?'

In the warmth of the Spanish evening, Malik signed the last of the official papers with a flourish and then handed them to Fariq. The brooding aide had been producing document after document ever since they had returned from dinner—but even the most tedious directives could not detract from Malik's his growing sense of excitement.

'No. Thank you, Fariq—that will be all. I shall take a drink on the terrace and then I shall sleep.' He yawned rather exaggeratedly, as if to impress on his aide a tiredness he was far from feeling. Not that he would usually

bother with subterfuge where a lover was concerned, but this lover was different—and propriety demanded that he be discreet about her.

'As Your Highness requires.' Fariq's face
showed no reaction as he bowed deeply and
left the lavish suite. 'I bid you a comfortable
night, Most Serene One.'

Malik had been given the entire top floor of
the luxury Madrid hotel, and his own private
quarters consisted of a vast two-bedroomed
suite connected by a shared drawing room.
There was a separate study, from which he
could work, two separate dressing rooms and
two bathrooms. The place had been chosen especially to appeal to his tastes. There were
Moorish-style towers on this particular
building, and cool marble floors. Sandalwood
hung on the air, and huge embroidered
cushions lay scattered on the floor of the salon.

Silk robes shimmered as he stretched his
arms above his head and walked outside onto
the rooftop terrace—a fairytale haven lined

with orange trees which scented the soft night air. Fat candles guttered in the faint breeze and bright stars hung in the sky like celestial lanterns, while far below came the glitter of a city still awake—but Madrid had always been a city that never slept.

Glancing at his watch, his eyes gleaming with anticipation, he walked back into the apartment just in time to hear a light tap on the door.

'Come,' he murmured, and in walked Sorrel—exactly as he had commanded that she should do when he had bent his head to speak to her at the end of dinner. In the soft light her face was a beautiful blur, but he could see its troubled expression.

A frown appeared between his black brows. 'What is it?'

She tried a smile, but it fell short of the real thing, and beneath her breast her heart was pounding. 'I feel sort of guilty, sneaking around like this—it seems so *wrong*, somehow.'

Malik's frown deepened. 'What does?'

'All the secrecy.'

'You *knew* it would have to be secret.'

His voice sounded reproving, and Sorrel swallowed down some of her reservations. 'I know. It's just…well…'

'Well, *what*, Sorrel?' he asked coldly.

Wasn't it pointless to tell him that ever since the sumptuous dinner hosted by the Kharastani Ambassador had ended she had been pacing up and down in her room in an agony of nerves—wondering how she was going to go through with it? Wondering if she had taken leave of her senses to ever agree to such a scheme.

I'm scared, she wanted to say—except that she suspected it would place too heavy a burden of responsibility on Malik's shoulders. It had been *her* decision to become Malik's lover. If she acted like a child, then he would treat her like one—and wasn't the whole point that she wanted him to treat her like a woman?

'I didn't know what to do,' she admitted huskily. 'Or what to wear.'

This was better. A few first-night nerves were permissible—as long as she had not changed her mind. Because Malik most certainly had not. His black gaze scanned over her with economic efficiency as he remembered the lavish evening they had just spent.

During dinner she had served him well—an excellent example of how perfectly a Western woman had adapted to life in such a radically different country as Kharastan.

She had looked magnificent, too—more magnificent than he could have ever dreamed, transformed into a ravishing beauty. There had been a split-second of disbelieving silence when she had walked into the crowded reception room just behind him, as part of his entourage. The Embassy had, of course, received word that Sorrel would be among his party—but he suspected that her youth and her pale blonde loveliness had taken the assembled hordes by surprise.

Her long, fitted dress, in scarlet embroidered

with silver, had caused a stir, and he had seen the envious eyes of the other women calculating the cost of the exquisite emerald clips she wore in her hair and the long emerald drop earrings which glittered in green waterfalls by the side of her face. Malik had even caught a visiting British politician trying to sweet-talk her during the pre-dinner drinks.

'I did not realise that Kharastani women wore scarlet,' Malik had heard him say.

And Sorrel's cool reply. 'Perhaps you aren't aware that I'm as English as you are—and scarlet does not have the same connotations in Kharastan as it does in the West. For us, red denotes courage and fertility—not loose morals.'

Malik had watched with amusement while the man's mouth had opened and shut like a fish, and Sorrel had moved away with grace and charm to get ready to meet the Castilian Duque and his wife, who had just entered the grand reception room of the Embassy.

Yes, Sorrel had been a worthy addition to the

Sheikh's party, thought Malik with satisfaction. Even Fariq must have seen that—and, although his aide clearly disapproved of the situation—Malik knew that he would not dare to express his reservations to *him*.

'You did well this evening,' said Malik softly.

'Did I?' She had felt a bit like a performing seal—brought in to cleverly balance a ball on the tip of its nose without dropping it. Sorrel had been raised by diplomatic parents and had attended similar parties since she could remember. She wasn't worried about what to say, or drink, or even do—because it came to her as easily as breathing.

What had been different this time were the circumstances in which she'd found herself. She had been aware of the ripple of interest when she'd walked in, and of the jealous glances sent slanting over by the other women in the room. Malik was known in the Press as one of the world's most eligible bachelors—and Sorrel suspected that a lot of those women had dressed up wondering if they might be lucky enough to be able to snare the ruggedly handsome Sheikh.

'You know you did,' said Malik, but with a renewed sense of impatience. Was she going to need reassurance every step along the way—when he was busy himself with paperwork from back home which still needed the royal seal, as well as all the trade negotiations he and his team were making during this whistle-stop trip? She must learn quickly that as mistress to the Sheikh she was there to make his life easier—not to complicate it with her own issues. 'Now, stop frowning and come over here.'

Her momentary feeling of shyness was overcome by the smile on his dark face and by the thought of how long she had yearned for him. Sorrel went to him with all the greedy eagerness of someone whose aching hunger was just about to be fed. He hadn't touched her since they'd left Brighton, and she had had to endure the formality of arriving in Madrid and wondering whether she had imagined the whole bizarre pact they'd made. 'Oh, Malik,' she whispered, and flung her arms around his neck.

The breathy way she said his name set off little warning bells in the recesses of his mind, and Malik caught her by the elbows to steady her, but also to restrain her. His exuberance was sweet, but it was not appropriate. 'Take it easy,' he murmured. 'I'm not going anywhere.'

Her head jerked back at the soft reprimand, and unthinkingly she bit her lip—but that did not please him either.

'Don't,' he chided. 'Your lips should only ever be bitten by a man—when sex becomes wild and angry and exciting, as sometimes it does. But they are far too soft and sweet and inviting for that. Especially not tonight. So this is better…' And he grazed his mouth over hers, gently and caressingly—the merest brush of flesh to flesh, which made Sorrel shiver as violently as a leaf about to be torn from the tree by a storm. Malik smiled against her. 'Ah, yes—this is much better. Now, relax. Hold on to me, but gently this time.'

Slowly, she raised her hands to lie on the broad bank of his shoulders, feeling the hard contours of muscle and bone through the silk of first his robe, and then his skin. It was a careful and considered movement—lacking all the impulsiveness of before.

Was that why he rewarded her by deepening the kiss? Making a little groan as their mouths opened together—so that the perfect synchrony of the kiss seemed to mock at her. As if he was saying, Don't show any *emotion* and I will reward you like this.

Okay, then—she thought. I won't. I will be as cool as you want me to be, Malik—I will bite back my words of adoration.

Yet although the kiss fell short of what her girlish dreams had once hoped for, on another level it exceeded every hazy wish she'd ever had. Because he *was* her every wish. Dark, powerful Malik was here—holding her and holding his hard body against her, exciting a response in her that came as easily as breathing, and she flicked her tongue inside his mouth with a luxuriant ease, as if she had been born to do that.

Her response took him by surprise—momentarily wresting the control from him so that for that one split-second he felt as if *he* was the pupil and she the teacher. 'Sorrel,' he said unevenly as he dragged his mouth away from hers, staring down at the wide-spaced beauty of her eyes and the parted dark petals of her lips.

'Do I please you, Malik?' she questioned softly.

She would please him more if she touched him where he was hard. But he knew that he could not ask her for such an intimacy—at least, not yet. Never before had such a familiarity been forbidden to him by self-restraint, and this, too, he found unbearably exciting.

'Oh, yes. Yes, you please me,' he agreed shakily. 'And you shall please me more. Come with me.'

He took her hand in his as if they were just any man and woman who could go where they pleased. But they were not. This suite—for all its opulence and luxury—was the gilded cage which confined their passions. And Malik confined them, too, Sorrel told herself as they walked in from the terrace towards his bedroom. With his rules about secrecy and appropriate behaviour.

She wanted to tell him that she was terrified—which she was—but she didn't dare, for fear that he would decide he'd taken leave of his senses and stop this madness before it went any further.

Because it *was* madness. And yet it was Malik on the only terms she could ever have him—and surely it would be madder still to turn down such a bittersweet opportunity?

'Now. Let me look at you.' He turned her to

face him, his black eyes almost grave as they studied her. Unexpectedly, he pulled out the emerald clip from the pale high-piled hair and carefully put it down, then removed another, and another—and watched like a voyeur as the abundance of blonde hair spilled in satin profusion down over the embroidered scarlet gown she was wearing. 'You must always wear your hair down for me, when we are alone like this,' he said huskily. 'Will you promise me that?'

She wanted to tell him that she would walk to the ends of the earth for him—but guessed that would be a far worse crime than hurling herself into his arms. 'I promise,' she whispered instead.

'And will you promise to tip your head to one side? Like that. There. Yes. So that I can brush my lips along your neck. Like this.' He felt the shiver of her skin, the faint tremble of her body as he did. 'Will you promise that too?'

Sorrel shut her eyes, the lids feeling heavy—

as heavy as the powerful beat of her heart. 'Yes,' she whispered.

'Your neck is like a swan's, Sorrel,' he breathed. 'Long and graceful. And you bend like the wind.'

She felt like a mannequin in a shop window, standing there with her hands down by her sides, while the soft touch of his mouth against her neck was making her tremble. 'Malik,' she breathed, unable to help herself, wondering if a shuddered hint of how much she liked it was overstepping the guidelines to behaviour he seemed to have laid down.

He pulled her into his arms and began to kiss her, and it was as much as Sorrel could do not to cry out in pure delight. It's only a kiss, she told herself fiercely. But it felt like so much more. A sweet, hot leap of her heart as his mouth covered hers. One minute his kiss was urgent and seeking and then, just when she thought that she might burst into flames, he would soften it—so that it felt like an unbearably evocative exploration.

And suddenly she didn't care about what was or wasn't suitable behaviour—because the kiss had ignited a passion which she had hidden away from him for years and years. Sorrel lifted up her arms and entwined them like a vine around his neck, hearing his answering moan as she pressed her body closer to his, and seconds later he tore his mouth away from hers.

His eyes were hot and black and his breathing was ragged as he sucked in a slow, unsteady breath—telling himself that he had to take back the control. The deal was that he would teach her all about lovemaking, and the best lessons were all about build-up. About enjoying each new pleasure along the way, rather than dulling the appetite by saturating it. Hadn't he told *her* off for being greedy? Swallowing down his alpha instinct to take her there and then, he bent his lips to her ear now. 'I want to take your dress off,' he groaned.

'Then t-take it off,' she said shakily.

In fact, he wanted to rip the damn thing from her body—but if he didn't calm things down then he would be lost, and Malik was *never* lost. He needed to demonstrate self-control—to prove to himself as well as to her just who was in charge.

He reached round to the side of her dress, drawing the zip down slowly so that the air cooled her skin, and even though it was like every fantasy come to life to have Malik's fingers brushing against the curve of her waist she sensed that something in the mood had changed. Now it seemed so…so *matter-of-fact*—whereas the frantic kissing had felt more…

More what?

More as if it really meant something to him? Oh, Sorrel—don't talk yourself into fantasy land, she told herself silently.

'Let me see you now,' he said.

He had finished unzipping the dress and was sliding it over her head, as if he undressed women every day of the week, and then he cast it aside and took a step back to look at her—like someone in an art gallery who was studying a painting in depth.

Sorrel's instinct was to blush and to wrap protective arms around herself, but something in his black eyes stopped her.

'No. You must not be shy with your lover,' he urged. 'For coyness has no place in the bedroom. Or out of it.' His eyes glittered. 'Now, take your hands away, Sorrel, and let me see you properly.'

Lifting them away, as if she were a puppet and he were twitching at the strings, she did as he asked and stood before him—like an early painting she had seen on the palace walls in Kumush Ay, of a favoured sexual slave in homage before her beloved Sheikh. Was that what she must look like? she wondered. A slave eager to do his every wish?

Searching his face, she found his expression unreadable, but she stood there while his black eyes swept over her simple lace-trimmed cotton bra and matching pair of briefs and he gave a hard smile.

'Go and look in the dressing room,' he instructed softly.

'What am I looking for?'

'You'll see.'

Coyness has no place in the bedroom, Sorrel reminded herself of his words as she turned and walked towards the dressing room—feeling his black gaze burning into her as if he was branding her with the hot fire from his eyes.

Malik watched her go, enjoying the delicious sight of each buttock thrusting against the cotton of her panties and the sweet, slightly self-conscious way she walked—despite what he had urged her. If ever he had doubted her innocence before, her whole demeanour since they had entered the suite had been one of a woman unused to men.

She didn't return straight away—and when she did it was with an expression he had never seen on a woman's face before. Of someone who was just discovering her sexual power for the first time. A sensual awakening. She had passed the first test and done what was expected of her, he thought with satisfaction.

'I assume that you wanted me to put these on?' she questioned.

'Oh, yes,' he agreed, and swallowed. 'Yes, indeed.'

Gone were the chaste cotton garments, and in their place the frivolous French underwear he had ordered in the very colour she had defended tonight at dinner. But here the scarlet did not symbolise the courage and fertility of which she had spoken. No, indeed. Here the flimsy little bra and panties were scarlet in their other more traditional sense—a colour which was totally about sex. Her breasts spilled out over the delicate lace and the high-cut briefs made her thighs seem to go on for ever and ever. Malik felt quite dizzy with desire.

It was as though he had never seen a woman dressed—or rather, *un*dressed—in quite such a provocative way. And maybe that was true. His lovers had stripped for him many times, but there had not been this sense of the new, the uncharted.

For my own eyes only, he thought—with a fierce stab of possession.

'Walk towards me,' he said throatily.

She obeyed him, finding that it was impossible to do anything other than sway provocatively on a pair of red killer-heels so high that she felt as if she was on stilts. This is crazy, she told herself—but a wild and delicious excitement whirled her up as she saw the look of sheer admiration in his eyes. So what if it's crazy? Why don't you just do the sensible thing and enjoy it?

'Like this?' She sashayed towards him.

'Yes,' he breathed. 'Exactly like that.'

But he had seen the play of emotions which crossed her face—the uncertainty and apprehension—and Malik was suddenly assailed by a terrible sensation of doubt. Was he wrong to be doing this? Taking the sweetly innocent and unspoilt Sorrel and playing these slow, sensual games with her? Was he *corrupting* her rather than broadening her education by teaching her how to delight a man and to delight herself at the same time? Knowing all the while that it could lead nowhere?

She reached him and gave a tentative smile as she flicked flaxen hair back over the gleaming silk of her shoulder. 'Here I am, then,' she whispered.

In that second she sounded so trusting—and so *sweet*—that the self-doubt threatened to overwhelm him. Until he reminded himself that if he were not doing this then someone else would be... The sharp spear of jealousy ruthlessly lanced the voice of his conscience.

Because if he didn't have her—then someone else would!

He picked her up into his arms in a display of strength and domination as he began to carry her towards the bed, and Sorrel closed her eyes. This bit really *was* close to fantasy—the stuff of a thousand girlish dreams—but most of the dreams had stopped at the bedroom door, and now panic had entered the equation.

She was about to lose her virginity in the most matter-of-fact way possible—to a man she had always loved, but who could never return that love.

Suddenly she felt the soft mattress beneath her back as he put her down on it, and her eyes fluttered open as she stared up at him, reaching her fingertips up before she could stop herself, touching the hard contours of his face and the grazing rasp of his jaw. Was tenderness forbidden, along with coyness? she wondered as she saw him flinch.

'Will it…hurt?' she asked tentatively.

And Malik gave a small groan—recognising the trust implicit in her question. The same trust with which she had once let him put her on the back of the palace's most feisty stallion, telling her that the only way to rid herself of fright was first to conquer it.

But this was a different Sorrel who lay on his bed—not the cute little girl who had been his ward for all those years. This was a grown-up Sorrel who was hell-bent on losing her virginity. Fiercely, he dispelled the memories of the past and concentrated on the glorious present—all soft, pale curves accentuated by sexy scarlet silk and lace—and he bent his mouth to kiss the tip of her nipple through her bra. 'No,' he said, his teeth teasing and grazing at the sensitised flesh. 'It will not hurt.'

Sorrel shivered with a wave of ecstasy so acute that it almost hurt. 'But I thought…'

He felt the rising tension in his own hard body. 'Then don't think,' he urged, his voice harsh from the recognition of just how difficult this was going to be. 'Thinking destroys pleasure, Sorrel—just feel.'

Her head fell back against the pillow as she did her best to concentrate on the waves of pleasure rather than the clear note of warning in his voice, which echoed round and round inside Sorrel's head like a tune she'd heard on the radio and found impossible to forget. Was that because thinking made you want to ask questions which would drive you mad if they were ever answered honestly?

But nothing ever turned out the way you thought it would. In her innocence, Sorrel had thought she'd lose her virginity to Malik that warm, orange-scented evening in Madrid—but the reality of the night was quite different. He didn't even undress her—well, not fully. Just reached round and unclipped the scarlet bra and then slowly removed it, flinging it carelessly to the floor as if it had been a rag.

He breathed out a long, pent-up sigh as her breasts were revealed, saying something soft in a word that Sorrel assumed was Kharastani, though she had never heard it used before.

'What does that mean?' she whispered,

trying to forget that she was lying there in a nothing but a wispy little pair of scarlet panties.

But Malik shook his black head, his tongue snaking out over bone-dry lips as he drank in the creamy beauty of her skin and the rosy blush of each nipples. 'It is not a word that a woman should ever use,' he grated, and he touched one tip with his finger, circling it with a light touch and meeting the question in her eyes. 'It means that you are ready to be shown the many paths which lead to pleasure,' he relented, and his mouth softened with promise. 'Ready to be loved.'

Sorrel closed her eyes to hide the sudden fear she felt. He meant *make* love, she told herself fiercely.

'Why do you frown, Sorrel?' he questioned softly.

She let her eyelids flutter open. How much should she tell him? How much of herself was it suitable for a woman to expose? Because suddenly the idea that she might lay her raw emotions open for him to see seemed far more revealing than the fact that her breasts were bare.

'I don't know what to do,' she said truthfully.

He gave a nod of satisfaction. 'But that is exactly as it should be. I do not expect you to. It is nature's way for the man to have superior skills and to teach the woman everything he knows.' A slow smile curved his hard lips. 'And, to be honest, it is a relief to have a woman who does not start performing her entire sexual repertoire in an attempt to impress me.'

She thought that it wasn't the most diplomatic thing in the world to tell her that at that particular moment, but the woman in her was curious. 'Is that what they do, then?'

'It has happened even more since I became Sheikh,' he admitted softly. 'For they believe that men can be ensnared by sexual expertise alone.'

'And can't they?'

He stroked a wisp of hair away from the

pink and white of her cheek. How innocent she was. 'Of course not. Sexual trickery is like food that has been messed around with—sometimes it ruins it—while simplicity has a charm all of its own.' Now it was his turn to frown—because what the hell was he doing, talking about such things with her? Was that not an intimacy too far—especially at a time like this? Because it was Sorrel—and she knew him better than anyone else? And did that mean she had some sort of power over him?

Never!

He renewed the stroking of her breast—only this time he ruthlessly decided to show her just what a master of expertise she was dealing with.

His fingertips teased, cajoled, excited, and his lips did the same. They traced feather-light patterns on her mouth, her eyelids, the tip of her nose and the gentle curve of her jaw, so that Sorrel relaxed into a hazy world where everything was about sensation. And through the haze she sensed that something wonderful awaited her.

Warmth began to flood through her as her heart picked up speed, and her arms reached up of their own accord to wrap themselves around his neck as Malik sweetly plundered her mouth with his.

'Malik!' she gasped.

He could feel the building of tension in her body, and he smiled as he slipped his hand between her thighs and began to stroke her through her panties, feeling her start. 'What is it?'

She wanted to ask him if it was possible to be feeling like…like… 'Something is…' Her eyes widened as the dark waves circled. 'Something is…'

He watched her as he might have watched a fledgling falcon taking its very first flight—then, as now, instinct was all. 'Don't think,' he said again, feeling the honeyed slick of her desire against his fingers. 'Just feel.'

Sorrel did as he urged, although there seemed no alternative, for by now the seemingly impossible waves of sensation dominated everything—taking her sweeping upwards towards a place of almost unimaginable pleasure.

'Oh, Malik!' she sobbed, as she reached it. 'Malik, Malik, Malik!'

'What is it?' he teased, instinctively laughing at her obvious delight.

For a moment all inhibition left her, and she stared up into the face of the man who had dominated her life since the first time she'd set eyes on him and her heart turned over. 'I love…' She saw the black eyes narrow and all the laughter leave them. Just in time she sensed his frozen withdrawal, and just in time she turned her sentence into a glowing sexual testimony. 'I *love* it,' she purred triumphantly, realising that at that moment she didn't sound like Sorrel at all.

CHAPTER EIGHT

YET just who *was* the real Sorrel?

Was she the woman who was being given a unique sensual education—who every night was brought to gasping orgasm by the silent and black-eyed Sheikh? The woman who bit back the words she knew he never wanted to hear—well, certainly not from her—and turned them into sighs of satisfaction instead?

Or was that just a temporary Sorrel, who was discovering sexual pleasure for the first time—rather as someone who had lived on another planet might greedily alight on their first taste of chocolate?

But the present didn't bother her nearly so much as what lay ahead. Because when it was over—as one day it must inevitably be—would she be able to walk away without a single pang and with a casual little wave of her fingers?

She couldn't bear to think about it.

'Sorrel!'

Just the sound of Malik's voice made her heart miss a beat—just as it always did—but she composed her face into one of calm attentiveness.

They were now in Paris—the last stop of the tour—and she had been reading through a clutch of newspaper cuttings, some from the French dailies and some from the international press. The Sheikh had been well received, she thought approvingly, putting aside her own feelings as she heard the sound of his distinctive footsteps.

'I'm in here!'

He appeared before she had time to adjust her hair, and stood framed in the doorway of their suite with his black hair gleaming and his ebony eyes glittering in the hard, autocratic face. It was a bright Parisian day and outside the weather was just glorious—though Sorrel thought that they might as well have been anywhere for all that they saw of the cities they took in.

They had been whisked from airstrip to hotel to Embassy by air-conditioned limousines whose windows tinted out most of the natural light—so that even if, as they had yesterday, they happened to see the Champs-Elysées passing them by, it was like looking at a sepia photo of it. A postcard image.

They were cut off from the rest of the world and cut off from reality in more ways than one. Sometimes the whole experience felt as if Sorrel had wandered into a dream by mistake—and never more so than now, with the fine golden silk of his gown shimmering around the hard sinews of a body she had yet to discover.

Sorrel shivered at the expression in his dark eyes. 'Did you…did you want something?'

'I want you,' said Malik softly.

And, oh, how she wanted him, too—but no doubt he knew that. Just as he obviously expected her to drop everything and rush to him. Straight into his arms. To hold her face eagerly up to his for a kiss and to tremble with anticipation at the guaranteed pleasure. Part of her wanted to do just that, but pride made her stay her ground to confront the issue which burned at the corners of her mind whenever Malik wasn't there to obliterate everything with his kisses.

How much longer before she completely lost her identity as a person—becoming solely Malik's plaything that he could pick up and put down at will? At least when she was busying herself by helping with practical arrangements for the trip it made her feel like the *old* Sorrel. The one who had existed before she had put her life on hold and her emotions into the deep-freeze while the black-eyed Sheikh took delight in showing her just how many ways there were to pleasure a woman…

'Well, here I am,' she said briskly. Because the role of aide fitted her far more comfortably than the role of would-be lover. 'I was busy with this itinerary.' She stabbed at the papers on the writing bureau at which she sat.

'Get Fariq to deal with it,' he said carelessly.

Her voice was stubborn. 'I'd rather deal with it myself.'

He walked over to where she sat and put his hands on her shoulders, bending down to brush his lips against her bare neck. 'But I don't want you to deal with it. Your place is with me. To do as I will you. To experience pleasure in my arms. You know that, don't you, Sorrel?'

Oh, yes—she knew that. She had learnt it at his lips and in his arms. Briefly she shut her eyes, allowing the warm whisper of his lips to lull her into the heady promise of what lay ahead. What would it be today? she wondered. Which erogenous zone would he be concentrating on—demonstrating his power and his skill in bringing her silently to gasping orgasm while somehow managing to remain both physically and emotionally removed from her?

The emotional distance didn't surprise her—she would have expected nothing else of Malik and she had known him all her life. But the other distance *did*—it surprised and shocked the hell out of her, and made her wonder if there was something the matter with her. Something about her which didn't please him, since—despite her growing sensual education and his masterly tuition—Sorrel remained a virgin.

At first she had thought that he was acting out of consideration for her feelings—imagining that she'd be scared because at the age of twenty-five she was a relatively late virgin. But she wasn't scared—she was longing for Malik to make love to her in the fullest sense of all. Yet he did not.

He would give her pleasure with his hands, or his mouth, or his tongue—and afterwards he would kiss her hair and let her shuddering body still within the safe and powerful circle of his arms. And then, when she was all rosy and contented, he would glitter her a hard smile and leave the room abruptly, leaving her satisfied and yet aching. Longing for more and not knowing why he would not give her more. Or *ask* for more. Was it about control? she wondered. Just as everything else in his life was about control?

Well, she certainly wasn't going to beg him.

She opened her eyes and slowly rose from the desk to face him. 'Your brother rang,' she said.

'My brother?' There was a pause. 'You mean my half-brother,' he corrected coolly. 'Which one?'

Which one did he think? 'The one who lives in Paris, Malik,' she said sweetly. 'Xavier.'

Malik didn't react, but went over to the window to stare out at the city's rooftops, narrowing his eyes against the glare of the day and keeping his body language neutral.

He had two younger half-brothers—Xavier, who was half-French, and Giovanni who was half-Italian. One father united the three of them—but their mothers had all been different. It was a complicated history, and one which Malik sometimes wished he could forget.

Up until two years ago he had thought that he was an orphan who had been lucky enough to have been given employment and protection by the royal palace of Kharastan. But the late Sheikh had made dynamite disclosures before his death: not only was Malik his son, and thus to inherit the Kharastani throne, but he was also going to gain two half-brothers.

On balance, Malik thought that taking on a kingdom was easier than taking on an instant family. He had been the Sheikh's right-hand man for so many years that he probably knew more about Kharastan than any other living person— and he had seen first-hand how best to rule.

The half-brother issue was different. Both Xavier and Giovanni were younger, and so there had been no question of them inheriting the Kharastan throne. Even if they had been older it was written into the constitution that only a man of pure Kharastani blood could inherit the kingdom.

The potential for discord between the three men had been there, but to his relief none had been expressed. Nonetheless, Malik had resisted the overtures of both Xavier and Giovanni for him to visit them and *'get to know them'*. He did not need a family and neither did he want one.

In his unique and often lonely role at the court, Malik had seen for himself that lives only became complicated when other people were involved. It was relationships which gave rise to unrest and to dispute. Relationships made you vulnerable—and exposed you to pain.

If Malik had not been King then he might have contented himself with a solitary life— like the one he had always led, the one he knew how to deal with. But such was not his destiny.

He could not take comfort in the luxury of choice. One day he must marry and produce an heir, but until that onerous burden should fall upon his shoulders he would give it no more thought.

He turned back from the window, thinking how magnificent Sorrel looked today—with her pale blonde hair tumbling down over her shoulders just the way he liked it, and in a long, white silk dress which fell in folds from the curve of her hips, so that she resembled a Grecian goddess. He felt his throat thicken with desire, but saw she was looking at him with a question in her eyes. He sighed. 'And what did Xavier want?'

Was he being deliberately imperceptive? Sorrel wondered. She put her head to one side and flicked a finger against her cheek as she pretended to consider the options. 'Let's think,' she mused. 'Xavier lives in Paris, and you happen to be visiting Paris. Any ideas what he might want—or shall we call in the palace logistician?'

His black eyes narrowed. 'Are you trying to be funny?'

'I thought you were.' She thought how forbidding his eyes looked—and how his lips were set into a hard line. But she refused to be intimidated by a man she had known all her life, no matter how much it suited him. She knew very well that he preferred to try to avoid issues such as these, and because she cared for him she wasn't going to let him. 'Malik—it's pretty obvious that Xavier and Laura want to meet up with you while you're in Paris! You haven't seen each other since Giovanni's party.'

He didn't need *her* to tell him when he'd last seen his brother! 'I don't know that there's enough time,' he growled.

'Oh, there's time,' she asserted softly, and pointed at his itinerary. 'The drinks reception with the Foreign Minister finishes early. You could easily do dinner.' She sighed as she saw that the forbidding set of his jaw hadn't altered a bit. 'Look, Malik, we've both known what it is to lose our families—but at least you've discovered a new one! Why don't you use this opportunity to get to know Xavier a bit better?'

She stood there, looking so at ease and so *comfortable* as she gently told him what to do that Malik felt a terrible tearing pain as he caught a glimpse of another life—a life he would never lead. Where women made suggestions in order to keep the peace and worked behind the scenes to bring distant brothers together. 'Will you stop trying to fabricate a situation which happens to fit in with your idea of Happy Families?' he snapped.

'I was *not*!'

Ebony brows were elevated into disdainful curves. 'Or perhaps you are hoping to present the two of us as a couple? Get the seal of approval from my family before you try to persuade me to tell the rest of the world we're together? Is that your plan?'

It was such an outrageous accusation that for a moment Sorrel thought he was joking—

but one look at the darkly thunderous expression on his face told her he wasn't. 'How dare you suggest that, Malik? When nothing could be further from my mind!'

'Because we are *not* a couple!' he clipped out. 'You know that and I know that—and what is more we never *can* be!'

'Of course I know that!' It was pretty obvious from the way he'd been hiding her away and…and… Her breath was coming in short, angry little gasps. 'You have made that abundantly clear!'

The conflict accelerated his heart and made his skin prickle, the dark flush of desire arrowing in slants down over his cheekbones. Wasn't it strange, he thought achingly, how disharmony could so accelerate desire? Anger provided an incomparable springboard for passion—which was why, he guessed, making-up sex was the very best sex of all.

The progress of his thoughts was rewarded with the hard jerk of an erection pushing against his thigh—but as always the physical evidence of his desire reminded him that this affair was different from any other. He had *made* it different—simply because it was Sorrel. He had held back and held back until he'd thought he would go insane—yet he wondered just how much more of this exquisite self-denial he could take.

'Come over here,' he instructed softly.

'No,' she said recklessly, but her heart was hammering against her ribcage. 'You think you can talk to me as if I'm an idiot, and then just snap your fingers and I'll come running?'

That was exactly what he thought. Well, not the idiot part, but certainly the rest of it. But he guessed it might not be the most diplomatic thing in the world to agree with her. 'Don't you know how much I like it when you try to oppose me?' he murmured. 'Don't you know how much it turns me on?'

Looping a strand of hair behind her ear, Sorrel stared at him. He had her tied up in so many knots that she wasn't sure about anything any more. *So ask him.* 'Malik—'

He heard the apprehensiveness in her voice—a trait that would not usually be made known to him—but then, he had never lived in such close confinement with a member of the opposite sex before. He was used to dealing with women at their glossy and most responsive best—all perfumed and ready for love. But the moment you let a woman into your life you became aware of her *moods*—and her unrealistic take on life.

'Come to me,' he ordered softly, and this time she went into his arms, her slim, soft body fitting perfectly against his. Unseen, he closed his eyes against the golden spill of her hair, breathing in its subtle fragrance before leaning back to look down at her, a stern expression on his rugged features. 'Now, tell me—what is troubling you?'

'You are.' Boldly, she lifted her hands to his face. 'You're driving me mad with questions about why…' She hesitated, and then seized the courage to say it. 'Why you don't want to make love to me.'

He traced a thoughtful finger down to the provocative swell of her breast. 'Isn't that what I've been doing to you for the past week?'

Surely it was crazy to feel embarrassed talking about sex when he had seen her writhing beneath his expert fingers and his lips in just about every major city in Europe? She hadn't felt embarrassed *then*, had she? Yet getting carried away in the heat of the moment was a lot easier than confronting difficult issues in the cold light of day, with a man who always ran away from discussing anything re-sembling feelings.

'I meant…properly,' she whispered, her face beginning to burn.

'Ah!' He stroked the palm of his hand over the pale waterfall of her hair, thinking that her stumbled questions reminded him of a butter-fly emerging slowly from the chrysalis before learning how to fly. He had seen her grow in confidence day by day. But that blush—redolent of a far more profound innocence—smote deep at the conscience which still troubled him.

Had he thought that one morning he was just going to wake up and find that the doubts which still assailed him over his behaviour towards her had suddenly vanished? That he would be able to take her—to pierce through to the very heart of her? And then what? To have his fill of her before casting her aside to seek a Kharastani bride?

Could he honestly, knowingly and willingly take her virginity at such a price? It was no way to treat any woman, but especially not Sorrel—not after everything they had been to each other.

And yet the alternative was to give her away to some other man!

Malik's mouth hardened. Never! His royal destiny had come to him late—but he'd now had two years of reigning over a large and influential kingdom, and some of that power had inevitably influenced him. He hungered for Sorrel with a fervour which far surpassed anything else he'd ever wanted. But he knew that he must not let sentimentality cloud his judgement.

As King he was above the rules of normal men, and this was fact, not arrogance. He could not, at present, see a way out of the dilemma which had snared him in its velvet claws, but until he did Sorrel would fit in with *his* plans and *his* desires. She would not question him, but consider herself grateful that he had taken it upon himself to educate her!

'You must not question my judgement—nor my behaviour,' he said coolly. 'Not ever. For I am the Sheikh, whose word must not be questioned!'

Maybe in matters concerning the body he was, but *she* knew a bit more about emotions and relationships than this cold-hearted King.

She drew a deep breath. 'Very well, I shall not bring the subject of our sex-life up again—I will bow to your superior knowledge of the subject.' Her blue eyes sparked. 'But I would be failing in my supportive role if I allowed you to take a course of action which could be detrimental to the throne,' she said quietly.

'Meaning *what*, precisely?' he snapped.

'Just that I think it's very bad if you don't meet up with your brother while you're here. If you won't do it out of a sense of love, then at least do it out of a sense of duty. Imagine if the papers discover that you've avoided him— they'll blow it up and turn it into a feud. You know the kind of thing: *Sheikh rivalry threatens Kharastan's stability! The full story of why Malik snubbed his half-brother.*'

For a second a smile caught the edges of his mouth before he could stop it, but he wiped it away and glared at her instead.

She dared to say *this*? To *him*? 'You are nothing but a manipulative minx!' he grated.

'Or a good mediator?' she countered, feeling that, yes, she was doing the right thing—but it was more than that. For once she was wresting a little of the control away from Malik— because surely it couldn't be good for him to have everything all his own way?

Malik's eyes narrowed. Maybe she had a point. After his unexpectedly dizzy rise to power the media was still engaged in finding out all about him—and how they would love to create a scandal out of nothing.

'Very well. I will see my brother,' he conceded slowly. 'Have security check and book us a table for dinner.'

Sorrel nodded and picked up the phone, speaking into it rapidly, all the time aware that Malik had walked over to the door which connected the suite to the corridor and was ensuring that it was locked before turning back and walking slowly towards her, his black eyes glittering. 'Now kiss me,' he ordered softly.

Her lips were dry and she needed no second

bidding, for she was hot and hungry for him—but her small triumph over the matter of his brother had filled her with courage. If she could assert herself over matters of state—then why the hell was she being so damned passive whenever he started making love to her?

She had been getting more and more emotionally frustrated by the one-sidedness of these erotic encounters—when Malik seemed to know exactly which sensual buttons to press and she just responded as if she'd been programmed to do so. But all the time he was so *removed*, so *distant*.

Maybe he took some kind of perverse pleasure in just watching her climax and then afterwards coolly walking away? Almost as if he were an observer in the act instead of a participant.

And maybe it's best that way, said a warning voice in her head.

Because you love him, don't you, Sorrel?

You love him, and he doesn't feel the same way and he never will—and maybe he's doing you a favour by staying emotionally and physically cold. Because at least it isn't filling you full of false hope.

Damn you, she thought suddenly, as he snaked his hand around her and began to rub at the indentation of her waist. At this point she would normally just sigh and let him kiss her over and over, until there was no option but to surrender.

Why *did* she always let *Malik* take control? Well, there *was* an alternative! Yes, she had gone to him untutored, but surely it would only reflect badly on the teacher if sometimes his eager pupil did not show some initiative of her own?

Luxuriously, she threaded her fingers in the jet-black waves of his hair and held her face to his. Her lips were soft on his in a slow, powerful and drugging kiss when unexpectedly she thrust her hips against his—a movement she had seen some of the court dancers perform. It wasn't the most subtle movement in the book, but it worked—because as she felt the unashamed hardness at his groin and slowly circled against it Malik tensed, black eyes wary, his fingers gripping hard at her waist.

'What do you think you're doing?' he demanded.

She rubbed up against him like an alley-cat, her hands daringly reaching behind his shoulders to massage the tension-knotted muscle there—touching him as she had wanted to do for so long, only had never before dared. 'Oh, Malik,' she purred. 'I think you know the answer to that!'

'Stop it, Sorrel.' He groaned, closing his eyes as she took complete command, pushing him down onto the soft pile of floor cushions as if he was her willing captive. 'Oh, please…stop it.'

'You know you don't mean that,' she murmured, slithering her hands beneath his robes and untying the silken string woven through the loose silk trousers which all Kharastani noblemen wore. Her movements were economical, because she did not want to give him a single second of opportunity for him to stop her. But just because they were swift it did not mean that Sorrel wasn't imaginative about this unforeseen seduction—heavens, no.

Malik had taught her much—that the body was made to be pleasured and that a man and a woman could find heaven on earth together.

How easy it was to touch him and make him moan. Not just because he had demonstrated such finesse towards *her* but because she *wanted* to please him—as he had pleased her, so many times.

She wanted to tell him how dear he was to her, how much a part of her life and her heart—but she contented herself with kisses and strokes instead, and hoped she hid her fast-mounting doubts as she slid the silk trousers off. How daunting the fully aroused sight of him, she thought! And how utterly magnificent.

'Sorrel,' he sighed, lying back almost helplessly—as weak at that moment as he had ever been. It was not the first time a woman had taken him in her mouth, nor the first time that he had been cupped with feather-light fingers at the same time—but usually he kept his eyes shut because the fantasy always superseded reality. This time he didn't.

He saw the movement of Sorrel's head, and the tresses of white-blonde hair spread out like a satin tablecloth over his thighs, and he felt himself coming. Considering that she had never done it before—he couldn't ever remember it ever feeling quite like…like…

Afterwards, she raised her head, and the sight of her sense of wonder—of delight at what she had done—nearly blew him away as much as the act itself. Her smile was almost shy—contrasting erotically with the magic she had just worked on him.

Warning bells went off in his head as she wriggled up, leaned forward and kissed him deeply on the mouth, and he moaned, because he could taste himself on her lips, and suddenly that felt like an intimacy too far.

'Sorrel,' he groaned.

Steeling her heart against her overpowering desire to sink into him, she rose gracefully to her feet, heading off towards the bathroom before he realised what was happening and could seduce her into staying.

Let him see how *he* liked it, she thought— as she ran the cold tap and thrust her wrists beneath it.

CHAPTER NINE

THE restaurant was at the top of a tall building which sat snugly on the side of the Seine and was reached through an impossibly glamorous lobby filled with flowers, its walls crammed with photographs of past politicians and film-stars who had dined there.

There were more photographs in the lift which took them up to the sixth floor. 'You're quite small fry in comparison,' said Sorrel, as she peered at a snapshot of a past president with the restaurant's owner.

There wasn't a flicker of response on Malik's face. 'Very amusing,' he said silkily, inhibited by the presence of one of his bodyguards—otherwise he might have kissed her. Or something. He wasn't quite sure what. For the first time in memory, Malik felt dazed and confused, and angry too. Had that extraordinary scene back at the hotel been a demonstration of Sorrel's newly discovered sexual power? he wondered. Or of control? She had played sexual games with *him*!

Because you played them with *her*? taunted the voice of his conscience?

The lift doors slid open and the bodyguard stepped out first, as protocol and safety dictated. Malik took the opportunity to bend his head to Sorrel's ear.

'You can wipe that triumphant smile off your sweet little mouth,' he grated. 'You may have won the temporary reprieve of a meal with Xavier and his wife—but I haven't forgotten what took place earlier.' Somehow he doubted that he would ever forget it—but that did not lessen his anger towards her. 'And we shall discuss it later. Alone.'

His words were coated with a dark danger

which made Sorrel's heart pound uncomfortably, but she kept her voice light. 'You make that sound like a threat, Malik.'

The black eyes glittered her a silent challenge. 'Do I? It's all in your interpretation, surely?' he questioned, and then there was a small buzz as he walked into the restaurant, with Sorrel trailing behind him.

Had she done something she was now going to live to regret? she wondered, as she followed in his dazzling wake. Played games with a man who liked to be in total control?

She could see heads turning, even though tonight he had elected to wear one of his beautifully cut suits. In theory, the Western garb should have made him blend in with the expensive clientele more than his robes ever did—but somehow it didn't. His tall figure was striking no matter what he wore—his jet-dark hair and olive skin even more so—and the autocratic way with which he moved across the room told even the most casual onlooker that this was a man of power and authority.

Xavier and Laura were already seated, but they rose to their feet as Malik arrived, and the four of them greeted one another with the familiarity born out of the extraordinary circumstances in which they'd all met.

Sorrel had first encountered Xavier when he'd arrived at the Blue Palace—the first of the sons to be introduced to his father—and Laura had been the English lawyer who had accompanied him. Sorrel hadn't seen them for ages, and she thought how tired Laura looked.

She found herself looking closely at Xavier and comparing him to Malik to see if she could see any family resemblance—but in reality the two men were strikingly different. Malik's skin was darker than Xavier's, but then he was of pure Kharastani blood, and only their statuesque physique and glittering black eyes showed any real similarities between them.

Almost as if it were yesterday Sorrel remembered when Xavier and Laura's wedding had been announced to a country hungry for the continuity of its royal family—and to a world who wanted the inevitable glamour of a royal wedding.

The people of Kharastan had rejoiced in the marriage of the Frenchman to Laura 'with the sunset hair', and many had hoped that the newlyweds would choose to make their home there.

Instead, they had gone back to Xavier's native France, where they now lived in a cosmopolitan area of Paris—although they were in the process of building a beach-house in Kardal, on the shores of the Balsora Sea because, as Laura said, they wanted to build ties with Kharastan.

'Why did you not come to our apartment this evening instead of this fancy restaurant, *mon frère*?' asked Xavier with the glimmer of a smile, as he looked around the immaculately formal room with its dazzling bird's-eye view of night-time Paris and the perfect dome of the Sacré Coeur gleaming with light. 'I could have cooked you *moules*, and Laura could have shown off how well she has mastered *tarte aux pommes*! She is proud of what a French house-wife she has become—aren't you, *cherie*?'

'*Mais, bien sûr!*' said Laura, with the care-fully correct accent of someone who has learnt a foreign language as an adult.

How comfortably *domestic* it sounded, thought Sorrel, unable to suppress a brief pang of envy—but she saw Malik give the faintest of frowns, and wondered if it was Xavier's easy familiarity with him which had caused such disquiet. Did his sheikhdom and the icy barrier he had erected around himself mean that he wouldn't even let himself get close to his brother? At least it isn't just around *me* that he keeps at an emotional distance, she thought bitterly.

Malik shrugged apologetically. 'That would have been wonderful,' he said smoothly. 'But unfortunately my security vetoed it in favour of this place.'

'Only because it justifies their salary and they love the whole red carpet bit whenever you go out anywhere in public,' said Sorrel, flashing her blue eyes at him. Because she knew and he knew that he could have overridden their objections any time he'd wanted.

There was the tiniest of silences, and Malik saw a look being exchanged between Xavier and his wife. Were they surprised that the Sheikh should allow one of his aides to be so familiar with him? He certainly couldn't blame them if they were.

How dared Sorrel offer an implied criticism like that—against him and also against his staff? Who the *hell* did she think she was? Was that why she had outrageously seduced him earlier, against his better judgement—thinking that sex gave a woman power over a man like Delilah chopping off Samson's hair? Well, she was going to get a short, sharp lesson in just who was master!

They glared at one another as the wine waiter approached.

'So, what's it like accompanying Malik on his trip, Sorrel?' asked Laura, breaking the rather awkward silence and shaking her head as a bottle of chilled champagne was held towards her glass. 'No, thanks. Just water for me. Is he an easy man to work for?'

Sorrel's lips twitched as the two women's eyes met in a moment of perfect understanding. 'Protocol dictates that I cannot answer that truthfully in front of the man in question,' she replied demurely, and Xavier and Laura both laughed.

Malik, on the other hand, did not. He just sat back in his chair, surveying her with a quietly brooding look that was making her feel more uncomfortable by the minute. Well, if he'd wanted her to sit there mutely he should have told her so at the beginning!

'And how is life in Kharastan?' asked Xavier, after they had eaten oysters with raspberry vinegar and then creamy scrambled eggs topped with shaved truffles, which was a speciality of the famous restaurant.

Malik smiled. 'The country continues to develop—culturally as well as financially,' he said thoughtfully. 'Everyone is naturally jubilant about the new oil-field—but there is an archaeological expedition over from the States which I'm particularly excited about. They've brought up some exquisite pots and bowls. We're hoping to open a new museum at the entrance to the site—but first, of course, we need to improve the access road.'

'Sounds like you've been working hard,' said Laura. 'And what's it like for women now? Any big changes since I was last there?'

Malik's gaze came to rest on Sorrel's pink and white face, and he felt a terrible jerk of sheer excitement as he remembered just where it had been positioned earlier. It was, he realised with a start, the only time in his life that he had ever been out on an occasion like this—with family, and also accompanied by a woman he was being intimate with. Or nearly intimate with.

Usually he compartmentalised. Women were for sex and relaxation. They were diversionary. He tried and failed to think of any other he would have brought along to an occasion like this.

'Sorrel would be better qualified to answer that than me,' he conceded.

Sorrel met his eyes, knowing that—despite the tensions between them which lay simmering beneath the surface—as ruler of his country, she admired him utterly and absolutely.

'We are introducing the driving test for women,' she said softly. 'Which is long overdue. Malik…well, Malik fought hard for that.' His black eyes mocked her stumbled compliment, but she meant every word of it—and she had to bite back a great wave of sadness as she watched Xavier place his hand over Laura's. They were so in love, she thought—and not afraid to show it.

Whereas they…

No. Stop it, she corrected herself—because that was all fantasy. There was no *they* with her and Malik—it was all *her. She. She* was in love with him and always had been, and *she* was the one who had walked arrogantly and gleefully into a situation which was now threatening to self-destruct. Like a tiny kitten challenging a fierce lion she had told him she wanted a lover, and he had called her bluff—but none of it had worked out. Why, they weren't even lovers!

She suspected that Malik had been holding back from full sex in order to give her time to retract her agreement and change her mind— because there was a part of him that always wanted her to remain sweet and pure Sorrel in his eyes.

He had held back with the kind of iron-hard restraint that she couldn't imagine in anyone else. But now she had probably blown it by seducing him. Such a proud and virile man would now surely take what he must consider to be his by rights. She could read it from the edgy and restless look in his black eyes when he looked at her—tonight he intended to finally take up her challenge and make love to her in the fullest sense.

But instead of feeling excited, and eager for it to happen, inside Sorrel was eaten up with nerves. Because deep down she suspected that the final intimacy would spell the end for them—once she had given him that, there would be nothing left to give. Her virginity would be signed, sealed and delivered, and her relationship with Malik—such as it was—would be over. Her mystique would be no more and she would become just another in the long line of his lovers.

'Sorrel?' A voice broke into her thoughts

'Mmm? Oh, sorry, Laura—I was miles away.'

'So are *les toilettes*!' Laura gave her a searching smile. 'Shall we go and find them together, and leave these men with an opportunity to talk to one another?'

Sorrel nodded, rising to her feet—aware of

Malik's gaze burning into her and wondering if the simple sheath of black silk she wore which fell like a dark waterfall to the ground met with his approval.

Eyes followed the two women as they made their way across the restaurant, and Malik's were among them as he watched her go. In a room full of beautiful and expensively dressed women Sorrel stood out like the natural beauty she was—though he didn't like her dressed in that sombre colour.

He turned back to find Xavier watching him intently, and suddenly he felt stricken with a pang of guilt, recognising that Sorrel had been right—his preferred option *had* been to try and get out of this meeting. To act as if he had no family at all. Yet a part of him bitterly regretted that he hadn't got to know his father until the last days of years of his life. Wouldn't he regret it even more if he didn't attempt to forge a better relationship with his two brothers? And the fact that he was here at all was Sorrel's doing, he reminded himself. *She* had battled to get him here.

He raised his glass. 'It is good to see you again, Xavier.' And to his surprise he found that he meant it.

'*Et toi aussi, mon frère.*' His half-brother sat back in his chair, his eyes full of question. 'How I long to ask you a question that protocol would frown on,' he murmured.

'Ask me what you will,' said Malik gruffly. 'For are we not brothers?'

For a split-second their eyes met in a moment of pure kinship, and Xavier nodded in silent and grateful acknowledgement of the bond. 'Is it serious?' he asked softly. 'With Sorrel?'

'*Serious?*' Malik was taken aback. 'How the hell can it be serious?'

Xavier shrugged. 'I just felt that there was something…between you.'

'But we've been snapping at each other all evening,' objected Malik.

'Precisely,' said Xavier dryly. He glanced

towards the direction of the restroom and hesitated. 'You are lovers, perhaps?'

Malik sighed and shook his dark head. That depended on your definition of the word. 'No. For she is a virgin,' he said slowly, almost as if he had forgotten Xavier were there.

Xavier's black eyes narrowed as he looked at his half-brother. 'Ah! I see. Yes, I see,' he said slowly. He stared down at his hands for a moment—and when he looked up again his black eyes were clear and candid. 'Then you must leave her now,' he said. 'Or marry her.'

'I know that,' said Malik fiercely. 'Don't you think I don't know that?'

The women came back in time for dessert and coffee—though Laura refused the restaurant's famous chocolate mousse and just sipped at a cup of fruit tea instead.

In the lobby they said their farewells, and Malik agreed to visit them in Kardal, when their beach-house was completed. Amid the chatter of future plans Sorrel stood to one side—feeling left out and not knowing whether, if ever, she would see the couple again.

It didn't get any better once they were inside the limousine, because Malik seemed preoccupied and Sorrel sensed that some sea-change had occurred over the course of the evening. He did not touch her, nor even look at her—and there was none of the flirtation she had come to expect from him. Without knowing how—or why—she suspected that it was going to be over between them before it had even started.

But you do know why, she thought unhappily. *You have crossed over an invisible line. By seducing him you have discarded your pure and virginal identity and he will have lost respect for you.* And even though she tried to tell herself that she had been acting like an *equal*, instead of a submissive little yes-woman, it still hurt—and she still wished she could rewind the clock for it never to have happened.

Malik turned his head to stare out of the

window, where tourists wandered the streets as happily as if it was daylight. The car sped down the Champs-Elysées and skated the edge of the Trocadero—all floodlit, like a giant film set, with the watchful frame of the Arc de Triomphe in the background—but Malik saw nothing of these.

His head was full of conflicting thoughts as he balanced dreams against reality, desire against morality. By playing sexual games with Sorrel he now found himself in deep and dark swirling waters—not knowing which way the land ahead lay. If he took her virginity, then he would have to marry her. He hadn't needed Xavier to voice it for in his heart he had always known this. And yet now—as then—the same question reared its head. Was the price too high?

Wouldn't it be better for all concerned if he did what most men in his position would do? If he forgot all about Sorrel? If he played the field for a few more years and then settled down with a meek Kharastani wife who would allow him rightful dominance in his home as well as in his country? Not a woman he knew almost too well to be comfortable with, who was in turn feisty and manipulative and, with her English boarding-school education sometimes just too independent for her own good.

She chose just that moment to cross one leg over the other—so that he could see its long and shapely definition through the silky caress of the black gown she wore. He wondered if she was wearing stockings underneath, and swallowed down the sudden thickness in his throat. Could he bear never to penetrate her? Never to know that unbearably sweet sensation of completion with her—their contrasting rhythms finding sweet communion in the coming together of their bodies? His tongue snaked out over suddenly dry lips.

'Laura's pregnant, you know,' she said, searching around desperately to fill in the yawning silence.

Malik stilled, erotic thoughts swept away like leaves from a path. He frowned. 'She told you that?'

'She didn't need to—not at first. Because I guessed—didn't you? She wouldn't drink wine, and she looked so tired. I asked her if she was okay when we were in the loo and she told me.' She wasn't going to tell him that she'd almost broken down and told Laura that she was in love with the Sheikh. 'They haven't said anything about the baby yet because they're terrified of jinxing it—she had a miscarriage last year. Did you know that?'

'No,' he said slowly. 'I didn't know that.'

'But she's past three months, so it looks fine,' she added, then saw the dawning of a new burden which shadowed his dark face and wondered how she could have been so dense. Because for Malik it was not just cheery news that his half-brother was about to become a father. When you were royal the repercussions of a new life were even more significant than usual.

Xavier's baby would become the first of a new generation of the Ak Atyn family. He— or she—was its future, and would continue its line even if Malik were never to produce a child of his own. Would that make him feel threatened, she wondered, or under some kind of subtle pressure to lay the foundation for creating his own dynasty?

She stole a glance at the hard and rugged profile, but he sat silently, as if carved from some dark and immutable stone, seemingly oblivious to her presence.

Malik's head was buzzing—his mind filled with all the repercussions of his half-brother producing an heir. Was this the wake-up call he had needed to stop avoiding the issue which had been hanging over him ever since the golden crown of Kharastan had been placed on his head at his coronation?

As they let themselves into the suite, leaving the bodyguard standing on guard outside the heavy-duty door, Malik thought how quickly the focus of what troubled you could change. Earlier this evening he had been caught up with nothing more far-reaching than a tussle with his pride and a battle with his conscience. Whether or not he would take Sorrel to his bed for the night had been the question looming large.

But now—with the news that his half-brother was to become a father—his own very existence had been brought into the equation. Malik took his Sheikhdom very seriously—he had not been born to power and did not wear its mantle lightly. He was aware of its honour, and all its responsibilities, and these were what absorbed him now.

Should his first consideration not be to his people, rather than to himself? Were they troubled by the fact that he had shown no signs of settling down—when in fact most of his energies had been spent adapting to his new role and bringing Kharastan into the twenty-first Century.

Sorrel turned to look at him, and as she did so he was aware of the contrast between hair and gown—moon-pale and sky-dark—both gleaming as softly as stars. Her eyes were large and blue and very beautiful, and the curve of her hips spoke instinctively of the dual role at the heart of every woman: lover and mother.

Suddenly he forgot all thoughts of home as his other dilemma took shape in his mind. Because Sorrel had become a problem, and he was a fool not to have anticipated that this would happen.

He wanted Sorrel more than he had ever wanted any other woman in his life, but if he took her virginity he would have to marry her.

Yet he needed a wife!

As never before—he needed a wife!

Was this fate, interceding as it had done so many times before? he wondered. Was practicality enough reason to align their futures?

Yet if he didn't act, then he would lose her. Someone else would swoop in and take her—

for she was ripe and ready for love. Could he bear the thought that another man should know her intimately?

Seized with a certainty that this was the path he was meant to take, he caught her in the crossfire of his black gaze. 'Sorrel?'

She frowned, sensing something momentous shimmering in the air around them. 'Yes, Malik?'

There was a pause before he spoke. One of those pauses which seemed to go on for ever, like the moments before birth, or death. Life-changing moments. 'Will you marry me?'

It was the last thing in the world she had expected, and Sorrel was confused. She met his eyes, her own candid with question. 'Why?'

In a way he knew her too well to tell her anything but the truth. 'I need a wife.'

'Because of Laura's baby?' she questioned dully, wondering if the ache in her heart showed on her face.

'That's one of the reasons, yes.'

'And because of my virginity, presumably?' she asked him painfully.

He felt his body tense. 'That's another reason, yes. I cannot take it without offering you something in return—and I cannot contemplate the thought of another man being intimate with you.'

'Gosh, what a lot of reasons!' she said sarcastically. Jealousy, possession and expediency—they were what lay behind his proposal. He hadn't said a word about the way he felt—but maybe that shouldn't have surprised her. To Malik, she was a woman who had been prepared to barter her virginity—all he had done was offer the highest price.

Malik saw the cloud which had crossed over her delicate features, but now that the idea had taken shape in his mind he pursued it with the single-mindedness that he brought to everything. 'You told me how much you missed Kharastan, Sorrel—how did you describe it? Like there was a hole in your heart.'

Oh, the stupid man—didn't he realise that she had been missing *him* as much as her adopted homeland? 'I don't remember saying anything like that,' she said coolly.

'But you do miss Kharastan,' he said silkily. 'I can see it in your face whenever you talk about it. The dreamy look in your eyes.' His mouth hardened with resolve. 'I cannot think of a woman better qualified to help me rule—and just think what your father would say if he knew what I was asking you today, Sorrel, can you imagine?'

How clever and calculating he could be, she thought—he knew that those particular words would affect her in a way that few others could. Her father and mother's happiest years had been spent serving the country they had grown to love with a passion—a passion they had passed on to their only child. Malik had witnessed the close bond which had existed between her and her parents—indeed, at times he had seemed almost wistful about it, and Sorrel had said as much to her mother.

'That's because Malik has never known what it is to have a family,' her mother had said. Had that been another reason why Sorrel had always hung around him? Always delighted when she could manage to put a smile on that stern, handsome face of his? Was that the reason why her father had taken the extraordinary step of making Malik her guardian? Had such an unusual union been one of his own dreams?

No. Now she was just getting fanciful—but it was difficult to avoid it when that same Malik was standing in front of her now, with a question on a face grown harder and yet more beautiful over the years.

'I will ask you once more, Sorrel,' he said silkily. 'And then never again. Will you marry me?'

CHAPTER TEN

OF COURSE she said yes. What else could she say?

Sorrel had loved Malik since the year dot— long before he became his Serene Highness the Sheikh—and she loved him still. Despite his moods and his arrogance and his icy control, she couldn't just switch that love off like a tap—no matter how hard she might try.

Yet what could have seemed like a fairytale was most emphatically not. There was none of the romance or celebration or joy associated with such an occasion. They discussed it with the same kind of emotion with which they might have discussed the takeover of a business.

The first thing he did was kiss her—but it was

a perfunctory kiss, like the rubber stamping of a contract—and the next thing he did was ring for Fariq, who bowed and congratulated him with a face so shadowed that Sorrel couldn't tell whether or not he was pleased.

'Sorrel must be assigned another room immediately,' Malik said, and Fariq bowed once more and went off to do the Sheikh's bidding.

'Why?' whispered Sorrel.

Malik's black eyes narrowed. 'Because there shall be no more temptation before the wedding.'

Sorrel laughed uneasily. What better night to consummate their relationship than this, and get properly close to him? This had to be some kind of joke, surely? Then she saw his look of determination and realised that it was nothing of the sort. 'But what difference does it make now?' she demanded. 'We're engaged!'

'It makes all the difference in the world, Sorrel,' he retorted. 'For it is custom and tradition that the Sheikh should marry a woman who is intact.' He saw her wince at his choice of word, but it was too late to take it back. Her eyes were big and blue and appealing, and the look in them had the power to make him ache…

'Malik—'

He halted her with a fierce look, remembering how defenceless he had felt beneath the merciless onslaught of her hands and her mouth when she had seduced him before dinner. And he resented that feeling—just as he resented her for having caused it—even while his body shivered with the erotic memory of it. 'Don't even think about it,' he warned softly. 'I know that you want to demonstrate your new-found sexual confidence, and you will have every opportunity to do so, but it will have to wait until afterwards. I want to do this properly.'

'And if I disobey you?' She flicked her blonde hair back. 'If I come over there and take you in my arms?'

His black gaze was steady. She must learn two lessons: that *his* wishes were paramount and that she must never, *ever* disobey him. 'Then there will be no marriage—for no such contract will take place unless I can present the betrothal to my people with a clear conscience.'

'No one will actually *know* if I'm a virgin, Malik!'

'You will know. And I will know. And that is what matters. You will come to me pure and unsullied on our wedding night.'

He saw her look of hurt disappointment and steeled his heart against it. Because suddenly events felt as if they were overtaking him—as if the order he had created in his newly made life was in danger of slipping into chaos if he did not take control. His senses felt raw—as if the layers with which he protected himself were slowly being peeled away to expose the man beneath.

Malik swallowed down his desire, and the anger that she could make him feel this way—but most of it he put down to frustration. At least it wouldn't be much longer. He intended to order that the wedding take place as quickly as possible. His mind skated ahead. There would have to a few changes made in the laws governing his choice of bride—but what the hell? He *was* the law!

'Trust me, Sorrel—the wait will be worth it,' he murmured. 'By the time I take you to my bed it will far surpass all our expectations.'

She had wanted comfort and reassurance as much as anything else—though Malik seemed to think this was simply about sex. And yet could she really blame him if he did? After all, hadn't she behaved in a way which deep down he must disapprove of? Kharastani women were not brought up to think of themselves as sexual equals—and, while Malik might desire her with an intensity which had banished all reason, would he have any genuine respect left for her? When desire dimmed what would be left to sustain a marriage?

But it was too late for doubts—and royal brides-to-be weren't allowed to have them anyway. She had given him her answer and she must honour that.

And by the time they arrived back in Kharastan preparations for the wedding and the deluge of interview requests from the world's press meant that she didn't have a minute to call her own, so her doubts were pushed away.

She quickly began to realise that her life was going to be very different from now on.

Someone from her schooldays had sold a very unflattering photo of her wearing a pair of shorts to the newspapers—and people that Sorrel hardly remembered were suddenly coming out with old 'quotes' which she didn't recognise as the kind of thing she'd ever said.

Then there was the added pressure of a leak to the press that Laura and Xavier were expecting a boy. The first Sorrel knew about it was when she was giving a rare, pre-wedding interview and was asked, "Will you be trying for a baby straight away?"

It seemed that no subject was deemed taboo. Now that she was seen as a piece of public property her life had changed for ever. And things within Kharastan itself had changed, too—something she hadn't anticipated.

For years Sorrel had had the run of the palace, and felt totally at ease there. She had always swum in the Olympic-sized pool and petted the Akal Teke horses in the stables, wandered in the beautiful gardens and generally felt that it was her home.

Now she was watched. She was no longer just Sorrel—the blonde Englishwoman who had worked her way into the affection of the Kharastani people by virtue of her long association with the royal family. Now she was to become the Queen, and people began to be guarded whenever she was around. Gone for ever was the spontaneity and freedom of her life, and with hindsight she could see how much she had taken those simple pleasures for granted.

But she had accepted Malik without any

terms or conditions on her part. She had not asked for his love—probably because she knew he would not lie about it, or pretend to feel something he didn't. And the alternative— a life *without* Malik—was something she wasn't prepared to contemplate. Not now that she had tasted temptation in his arms...

Her face was icy with terror as she dressed for her wedding, and her isolation seemed to mock her once she had dismissed the maid-servants, afraid that emotion might get the better of her and that she might break down in front of them—an unforgivable crime for a Queen-to-be.

The immense silence seemed to deafen her, and it had been a long time since Sorrel could remember feeling quite so lonely as she did at that moment—which was ironic, really, given that she would soon have a husband. But it was at times like this that you really noticed the lack of a family—and Malik's words came back to her. Through the sudden blur of tears she saw her golden and scarlet reflection looking back at her from the mirror—wishing above all else that her parents could have seen her today, in all her wedding finery.

And Malik was right—how proud her father would have been that she was marrying the Sheikh.

Yet would Sorrel's perceptive mother have noticed the faint sadness which clouded her daughter's blue eyes? Or observed the very real anxiety which was making her skin feel cold and clammy?

The fear that she had leapt too hastily at Malik's unexpected proposal and was now worried that she was going to live to regret it.

How she wished that she had had the courage to ask her husband-to-be about just what kind of marriage he was anticipating.

But she had not had the opportunity to ask him—and now it was too late. The guests were assembled and waiting, and in an hour she would no longer be Sorrel, who didn't know where in life she fitted in, but Queen, married to a man who didn't love her.

A rap at the door interrupted her thoughts, and Sorrel opened it to find her two sisters-in-law standing there, carrying her bouquet which had been freshly gathered from the palace gardens that morning.

The two women had arrived with Malik's half-brothers a week ago, and Sorrel had been showing them the hidden treasures of the country while Malik locked himself away in his office to deal with the border dispute with Maraban and the constitutional changes thrown up by their marriage. He had made sure that they were never alone—and even at the formal dinners which had been held every night in the run-up to the ceremony barely more than a few words had passed between her and her fiancé.

Laura looked glowing—especially compared to the night Sorrel had seen her in Paris. Her sunset-coloured hair was woven with creamy stephanotis, and a jade silk coat-dress disguised all signs of her pregnancy. Sorrel wondered how she must have felt about the hospital leaking the result of her scan—but somehow it didn't seem appropriate for her to ask.

'Look at these!' exclaimed Alexa, Giovanni's wife, as she put the bridal bouquet down on a carved mulberry dresser. 'Aren't they the most beautiful roses you ever did see?'

'Mmm!' Sorrel picked them up and sniffed at them dutifully, but when she looked up it was to find Laura staring at her, and she wondered if she had seen her fingers trembling.

'Are these just normal pre-wedding nerves, Sorrel?' Laura asked softly.

'Well…' Sorrel flashed the smile she had been practising in front of the mirror all week, hoping that it would convince Laura as well as the rest of the waiting world. 'Does the word "normal" ever apply where the Ak Atyn family is concerned?'

Laura smiled back. 'I guess not!'

'Come on—we've come to walk with you to the ceremony,' Alexa said to Sorrel. 'Are you ready?'

Sorrel bit her lip. Was she?

Every woman dreamed of her wedding day, and Sorrel had lived out this fantasy many times. Of moving slowly towards Malik, her eyes downcast and her head weighted by the circlet of flowers which surrounded a diamond crown.

When she reached him, she looked up into his eyes—her heart leaping with love as she issued one last small prayer that he would be smiling the kind of smile that his dream-like counterpart always had. But her prayers remained unanswered, for his face was as serious as she had ever seen it—the black eyes flinty and cold.

Was he regretting it too? she wondered.

The *maulvi* began to read aloud the vows in the classic combination of the formal, the spiritual and the legal which was at the heart of every marriage ceremony, no matter what religion. Deeply profound words that Sorrel's shaky voice stumbled over once or twice as she repeated them.

They each sipped from the goblet of life—a thick and sweet mixture of pomegranate flavoured with something no one could pronounce properly, but which tasted a bit like Turkish Delight.

She shivered as Malik tied the traditional double loop of silver and black beads around her neck—supposed to protect the marriage against evil—and then they were man and wife at last.

The guests dropped deep bows and curtsies as she and the Sheikh passed through the high-vaulted room to a courtyard decked with garlands, where traditional lute players sat strumming by one of the smaller fountains.

Outside, they stood in the bright sunshine, and Malik raised her fingers to his lips.

'So you are my Queen at last,' he murmured, his face shadowed by the flowing headdress he wore. 'And although you have just promised to obey, I see that already you have broken your promise to me.'

Sorrel's eyes widened, startled, her fingers flying to her throat—hurt that his first words as her husband should be those of reprimand. 'I have?'

Malik's mouth curved into an odd kind of smile. How brittle she looked—as if she might snap if he took her into his arms. 'I was teasing,' he said softly. 'You promised to always wear your hair down for your Sheikh, remember?' His eyes glittered with dark sexual promise. He was wishing that he could take her in his arms and kiss her properly—but propriety must be observed. At least until they were in their bedchamber. 'But I shall unpin it myself later—when we are alone.'

She stared up at him, scarcely able to believe that she was now his wife. Wanting to pinch herself to check that she was really alive and not still dreaming. Wanting some kind of re-assurance that she hadn't just done the most foolish thing. 'Malik, I'm terrified of doing the wrong thing.'

'There is no need. I shall teach you—as I have taught you everything else.' He thought how long she had been forced to wait for the pleasure she craved, and sought to put her mind at rest. 'You are a sensual and willing pupil, Sorrel.'

Did he think that everything came back to *sex*? she thought in despair. Or maybe this was the punishment for young women who announced that they wanted a lover—afterwards they would never be taken seriously. 'I meant…I'm scared that people won't accept me.'

He tipped her chin up with the tips of his fingers and stared down into the beguiling blue shimmer of her eyes. 'How can you be?' he asked simply, shaking his head so that the flowers in his own headdress shimmered like butterflies in the bright sunshine. 'When you look so perfect, and everyone is so happy about our marriage.'

'Are they, Malik? Really?'

'*Yes*. Really. They have watched you grow and they have seen how much you love our country. Why would you know even a second of doubt about the ceremonies today, when you could almost write a book about Kharastani protocol?' He shrugged as he saw her still needing to be convinced. 'Oh, there will always be people who think that I should have married a woman of pure blood—but it is up to you to win their hearts and prove them wrong. You may look like a foreigner, but you certainly don't act like one. You'll be fine, Sorrel—but you must learn to disguise your doubts and to hide your true feelings *behind the patina of confidence. That is what your people expect of you—indeed, what I* expect of you. So, come, let us go and greet our guests.'

She took his arm and they walked into the feast to the sound of fanfare and the flutter of rose petals—both Western touches which had been ordered by Malik for his new bride. But for Sorrel the day proved to be something of an endurance test.

All those things he'd just said about having to hide her feelings—she'd known that was what she must do, at least on an intellectual level. She was aware that Malik did it all the time—certainly in public. But was he going to carry on doing it in private, too? Were the two of them allowed to *have* feelings—or was everything supposed to operate on some lofty, superficial level, where extremes of emotion weren't encouraged?

But you've made your wedding bed—and now you have to lie in it!

He had not forced her to marry him. He had asked her coolly and calmly and she had agreed. She had walked into the marriage as an adult—so she had better start behaving like one. No one got everything they wanted in life—maybe this was enough.

Their bedchamber was lit with candles and scented with cedarwood and amber—both rich and earthy notes, believed by Kharastani custom to enhance the fertility of every bride-to-be on her wedding night.

As Sorrel slipped the sheer cream organza gown over her head, she began to understand a little of some of these old rituals. Suddenly she understood the necessity behind Malik's insistence that she come to him untouched on this significant night. She was the wife of the King—of *course* she must be pure.

'Sorrel?'

She heard his soft, deep voice—rich as honey, with its distinctive accent which never failed to send shivers down her spine—and turned to see him standing there, shimmering as if lit from within, in his cloth of gold with his belt and his sword slung around the narrow line of his hips.

'Yes, Malik,' she whispered.

He walked over to her, cupping her face in his hands and then touching them to the intricate confection of her hair, still crowned with the diamond circlet. 'I want to unpin your hair,' he said, his voice unsteady.

Carefully, he lifted off the glittering crown and laid it down, and then he set about removing the pearl pins, one by one—so that her hair began to tumble down around her shoulders, strand by strand. It was slow and sexual and highly symbolic of what was about to come. It was like every fantasy come to life—Malik, her husband, his handsome face focussed entirely on the task in hand. When her hair was finally freed he ran his fingers through it greedily—like a man who had dis-covered treasure.

'I have dreamed of this moment,' he said softly.

So had she. But now that it was upon her Sorrel felt stricken by a terrible shyness. This was no longer an erotic fight for equality in a Parisian bedroom, but an ancient submission of wife to master.

It was a union fuelled by convention, and by Malik's urgent need for an heir—but it would never be fanned by the flames of love. And yet surely that did not preclude a kind of tenderness between them—the kind that could never have existed during the cold-blooded arrangement of her sexual education? Did their long-standing friendship not count for something in the bedroom?

'Malik,' she whispered.

'Ah, Sorrel,' he said, his voice roughened with the urgency of self-denial. He had wanted her so badly, and for so long, and yet he knew that he must make this memorable for her, since it would colour her opinion of sex for evermore. But, by the desert storm, he was aching!

'Do you know how I have hungered for this moment?' he demanded. 'How night after night I have thought of this—and you—naked and pale in my arms and in my bed? And you have thought of me in the same way,' he stated with satisfaction.

'Y-yes,' whispered Sorrel, but there was something fierce—almost savage—about his dark features which made him look almost like a stranger.

'I think you're wearing too much,' he murmured. 'I think we both are. Ah, the sweet pleasures of disrobing! Shall I take this off?' His finger brushed over the diaphanous material of her nightgown.

'Y-yes,' she said again—and wondered where that *über*-confident Sorrel had gone— the one who had seduced *him* with such panache. Had the magnitude of their wedding day somehow inhibited her?

Laying her on the bed, he peeled her nightgown off and then began to remove his ceremonial robes. He had seen most of her body before—though never completely bare, always insisting on some wispy little thong or a pair of French knickers being worn, as if to conform to some ancient idea of decorum. But—apart from that night in Paris—there had only ever been one occasion when Sorrel had seen Malik partially unclothed.

It had been when she was still a teenager, and she'd come across him sword-fighting in the courtyard, with one of the grooms. The sight of his bare, hard torso—sheened with sweat and grimy with dust—had imprinted itself on her mind and fuelled her fantasies for years to follow.

But now, as he removed his robes, nothing could have prepared her for the magnificence of his naked body—with all its daunting strength and latent power.

In the candlelight his honed flesh gleamed, all golden and shadow, and Sorrel's fears multiplied. She wanted to tell him that she had been acting out when she'd said she wanted a lover—and that the last thing she had expected was for him to call her bluff. She wanted to say something as corny as *Please be gentle with me*—but she didn't even know whether he'd hear. Because now his face looked as if it was a tight, hard mask—it was if he wasn't really there with her, or maybe that he just didn't see her.

'Malik!' she gasped, as he climbed onto the bed and their warm flesh met.

'Sorrel.' He began to stroke her body, holding himself in check as his fingers began to tiptoe over her soft flesh. 'Sorrel,' he said again, more fiercely this time.

As a lover he was textbook perfect. He knew when to incite and when to retreat. The first thrust hurt—but that seemed to please him, for he gave a low laugh of almost indulgent pleasure. And afterwards it didn't hurt at all—he made sure of that. How perfectly he built the wall of desire, brick by brick, his lips in her hair and over her breast and in her mouth. She felt his body hardening inside hers, and suddenly she could bear it no longer and tumbled over the edge, her body convulsing over and over again.

'Malik, oh, *Malik*,' she groaned.

Sorrel was no stranger to orgasm—Malik had made sure of that too—but this time was different. This time it felt as though she would never be the same person again afterwards. Perhaps because his own sharp release came almost immediately, and she heard the ragged groan which sounded as if it had been ripped from the very core of his being.

Afterwards he withdrew, and kissed her hair and stroked her damp brow, but it was the same kind of perfunctory kiss with which he'd sealed their engagement, and which told her his thoughts were elsewhere. As if *he* were elsewhere. He rolled away from her and onto his back. Suddenly the space between them on the divan might have been a million miles. Was this what happened afterwards? thought Sorrel with a newly rising tide of panic. Did the joining of their bodies cease once they had been greedily fed with satisfaction—and why had it left her feeling *empty* inside?

Because he doesn't love you as you long to be loved, as you love him. And being Malik— hard, precise and perfectionist Malik—he wouldn't go through the pantomime of saying the words unless he really meant them.

Sharply, Sorrel bit her lip—tasting the sudden salt taste of blood and blinking rapidly in an attempt to keep her tears at bay, wondering if he could hear the tiny shuttering sound her eyes made.

Malik lay staring up at the ceiling, but he saw nothing of the dancing light show provided by the guttering candle flames. He thought of the long road which had carried him to where he found himself now. Brought to the palace by a white-faced midwife who had heard rumours of his progeny, taken in by the Sheikh but brought up by servants, never acknowledged as his heir until soon before his death.

For Malik, life had been a series of tests, of hoops to jump through. For most he had been guided by example—on others he'd relied on instinct. But relationships were the most tricky of all—and never more so than with Sorrel. Yet just for now all those minutes and months and years which had ticked by to bring him to just this point culminated in a perfect moment of peace. And he closed his eyes and fell asleep.

She lay, frozen with disbelief, until the soft and steady breathing of the man who lay beside her told her that she was not mistaken.

Malik was asleep!

The emotions which had been simmering away inside her for so long finally bubbled up to the surface and she felt tears beginning to slip from the corners of her closed eyes. She swallowed them down, but she could feel them rising again—like a rock pool when the tide started to pour in. In a minute she would wake him—and could she bear to have Malik find her crying on her wedding night, demanding to know why?

Sliding from the bed, she shivered a little as her bare feet touched the marble floor. Unaccustomed to her nakedness, nonetheless she did not dare risk pulling her discarded nightdress from the mattress and waking him.

But at least the night air was warm, and she blew out a couple of candles along the way, before going over to stand by the long windows. Their shutters were open to the beautiful palace gardens, and the moon was big and fat and full in the sky—but then, the wedding had been planned around the glory of its cycle, since a full moon was considered an auspicious omen in the Kharastani culture.

Honeymoon.

Oh, how the word mocked her! The tears rose in the back of her throat and she choked them back, but it was too late—for the dark figure on the bed stirred.

For a moment Malik experienced the split-second of disorientation which came between waking and sleeping. His senses were keen and ever-alert—he had spent long nights of vigil in the desert as part of his passage from boy to man. But snakes and scorpions and the crackle of a larger predator in the distance were threats he could deal with.

His new wife crying on her wedding night was not.

In the half-light, he frowned before he spoke. 'I believe that many women cry after the first time. They say that orgasm is a little death.'

Sorrel didn't turn, just nodded her head so violently that her hair fell all over her face. Her shoulders were shaking. 'Yes, that must be it!' she sobbed. 'It *must* be a reaction to sex! Because *that's* what's important—isn't it, Malik?'

Malik was outraged. 'That is rich, coming from you!' He sat up, the rumpled sheet falling around his hips, to see Sorrel carved in moonlight, her womanly curves like a silvered violin and her hair streaming down her back like white gold. But he hardened his heart against the dip in her back, the way her bottom curved into such perfect symmetry.

He spoke quickly and asked the question—before she could turn round and bewitch him with those big blue eyes. Even though the room was dimly lit there seemed to be no known antidote to her particular brand of enchantment.

'You are unhappy?' he grated.

'Yes!'

'Perhaps you regret having married me?'

'Yes, Malik!' she cried again, and the words broke loose from the dam inside her. 'Yes, I do!'

CHAPTER ELEVEN

FOR minutes there was silence—broken only by the fading sounds of Sorrel's crying, gradually becoming more muffled as her sobs grew less. She could hear the flick of a match and see a sudden increase of light as he must have lit a candle behind her. And because she couldn't keep standing with her back to him she turned round, expecting the fury on his face but still recoiling from its dark ferocity.

'Wouldn't it have made more sense to have thought about this *before* the wedding?' he snapped.

Now Sorrel felt even more vulnerable— naked, and facing the contempt which radiated from the powerful frame in waves so strong that she could almost see them. Sucking in a breath which still shuddered from her tears, she walked over to one of the low divans, where the golden lace veil she had worn for her wedding lay, and she picked it up and tied it around herself, knotting it like a sarong.

'I thought… I thought…'

'No—that's just it!' he stormed. 'You *didn't* think! If you had these kind of…*doubts*—' he fixed on the word exasperatedly, wanting to bang his fists in frustration against the wall '—then you should have shared them with me!'

She wanted to say that it had been difficult to share *anything* with him when they had been living on opposite sides of the palace and kept apart by convention. But even if they had been together would she have had the nerve to tell him how she really felt? Since when had Malik ever invited her confidences?

Malik's mind was racing. He had chosen Sorrel as his bride *despite* the fact that she was not native to his land—because part of him admired her adaptable character which her unique upbringing had helped forge. But when it came to the crunch she was *not* a Kharastani—and she was not constrained by the deeply-engrained values of that land.

Whereas a Kharastani would sooner walk barefoot over the burning desert sands than give up on her marriage—why, a Western woman would terminate such a sacred union as ruthlessly as the falcon swooped down to seize its bait.

As Sheikh—and as a relatively new and untested sheikh—it was his role to lead by example. What a fool he would look if his marriage was dissolved before the rose petals had been swept from the palace courtyard.

But Malik knew better than anyone that the only way to defeat fear was to confront it. Face your own worst nightmare and come through it and what else could possibly hurt you? At least, that was the theory.

'So you want to end the marriage?' he demanded.

Sorrel gasped. Was that how disposable an asset he saw her? 'Do you?'

'Of course I don't want to end the marriage!' he raged. 'My reputation will be in complete tatters if I do!'

The hope which had flared in her heart died a spectacular death, and Sorrel bit her lip. 'Well, we can't have *that*, can we?'

His instinct was to lash back at her verbally, to hide his hurt and his outrage that she should speak to him in such a way. But behind her sarcasm he heard the tremor of her own pain, and he stared at her—feeling as out of his depth as a non-swimmer who had just been hurled into the watery stew of the Balsora Sea in winter time.

Because Malik knew little about women— save for the very obvious stuff about how to please them in bed. The servants who had tended him during his growing-up years at the palace had wanted to adore him, but the proud little boy had always kept himself apart—had held something back. Perhaps it was being the product of a union about which there had always been whispers and rumours that had made Malik always feel as if he were floundering around in the dark. And when your mother died in childbirth people tended to pity you—and pity had been the last thing he'd wanted. Sorrel hadn't pitied him. She had been kind and she had been sweet—but somewhere along the way that sweetness and kindness had fled. He had taken them away, and left her with only hurt and anger.

His voice was sombre. 'What is it that you want, Sorrel?'

She could tell him that she wanted his love—but that would be like a child demanding a golden coach to travel around in, like the one Cinderella had. You should only ask for the achievable—and no one ever guaranteed that your heart's desire would be achievable.

'I'm afraid that we're going to have a marriage like your father's,' she admitted, giving voice to a concern she hadn't even known existed until now. 'With you travelling the world and making love to different women and siring babies by them.'

Had she alighted on that to wound him? Because wound him it did—but it was the pain of having a long-neglected and deep wound being hacked open before being cleansed by something harsh and antiseptic, allowing it the conditions in which to heal.

'My father did what his people wanted of him at the time,' he said simply. 'His wife, the Queen, was barren—and the country desperately needed an heir.'

'It still does.'

He didn't say *But we might have children of our own,* because somehow it seemed inappropriate—like a vision of a future that you might never have. 'Xavier is carrying on the next generation,' he said firmly.

'I thought that rivalry over *that* was one of the reasons you asked me to marry you.'

From anyone else this might have sounded like a criticism—but then, no one else would have said it, especially at a time like this, when their brand-new marriage hung precariously in the balance. This was Sorrel as he knew her best. Reminding him of what was real and what was not.

'It was,' he admitted. 'But maybe it wasn't enough. Like your virginity wasn't enough.'

And now Sorrel was properly scared. It was one thing for her to express her doubts—but quite another when Malik did it back to her. Because women verbalised while men *acted*, and it sounded as if….as if he really *did* want to finish it. A tight, cold dread clamped its way around her heart. 'What do you mean—it wasn't enough?'

For the first time in his life he felt helpless. Even when his suspicions about being the Sheikh's son had crystallised into fact he had not felt like this. As though he was being swept down a fast-raging torrent which used to be the trickle of a stream.

'I just wish we could have back what we used to have,' he said simply.

Sorrel stared at him. 'And what was that?' she whispered.

'It used to be so easy between us,' he said. 'I liked knowing you were there—only I didn't realise that until you'd gone.' He shrugged, like the little boy who had never been allowed to be just that. Who had always been told to behave like a man. It was the earliest lesson he had learnt—that men didn't show emotion—and there had been no loving mother around to tell him that they could.

'Maybe it was the sex that complicated our relationship,' he said slowly, when still she didn't speak, just continued to look at him with those big blue eyes, and in them an expression he didn't know. 'But I wanted you so much, Sorrel. When I walked into your flat and saw you looking like a tramp…' His voice was husky, his eyes opaque with remembered lust. 'I suddenly realised how much I wanted you.'

'Malik,' she said urgently—because she knew that she couldn't carry on holding back in case she got hurt. Because half-truths could hurt just as much. He might not feel the same way about her, but he needed to know what she felt for him—because surely it was churlish and unkind to hold back on emotions simply because you wanted something for yourself?

'I was crying because I love you,' she said quietly. 'Just the way I've always loved you. That's why I went away—because you seemed to look right through me and because I was projecting into an unbearable future, when you would take another woman as your wife. And I couldn't take it. I was crying because you will never love me back in the same way—and because I would never be able to tell you how I feel about you.'

His eyes narrowed suspiciously—like a wild

horse the first time it was offered food from the bowl. 'So you don't want to leave me?'

'Of course I don't,' she whispered. How could he honestly believe that? she wondered. But in the same moment she recognised that Malik didn't know how to receive love—probably because he'd never had any experience of it before. 'Never, never, never,' she affirmed ardently.

A sigh escaped his lips and she touched her fingertips to them, her eyes searching his face. And written there she could see the glimmer of something she dared not put a name to—but it set off the distant clamour of hope deep in her heart. In a way they were very similar: two outsiders, who blended in wherever they needed to but had never made a place of their own.

She loved Malik, and she wanted him to love her back, but one wasn't dependent on the other. She suspected that most of the ingredients were in place—he just needed to work out his own particular recipe.

But in the meantime she could show him hers. Show him with all her heart how love could be. She would be his partner in every way that counted—if he would let her.

'I love you, my darling Malik,' she said. 'I love you so very much.'

And Malik felt the sting of tears as he recognised that she had humbled herself before him—had not been afraid to put her feelings on the line. It was as if a veil had been lifted from before his eyes, and everything suddenly became clear.

There was a word to describe the way he'd missed her, the way he'd wanted her, and the way he'd felt as if his heart would break into tiny pieces if she ever went away again.

The lump in his throat made speaking difficult, but the word seemed determined to be spoken. 'I love you too, Sorrel,' he said, and then he repeated it. 'I *love* you.'

There was wonder in his voice as he let this brand-new emotion of love flood in—like sunlight streaming into a room which had always been dark before—and other emotions quickly came following in its wake. Joy. Comfort. Belonging. And longing. Oh, yes—there was longing.

But even the longing felt different as he cupped her face gently in the palms of his hands and looked down at her. 'Sorrel?' he said, almost brokenly.

'Malik?' she questioned, and the wonder she'd heard in his voice was now echoed in her own one-word question.

He bent his head so that their lips were almost brushing—their warm breath mingling, their gazes locked—and just in that moment before he kissed her his eyes gleamed with sheer delight, even as his body hardened as never before.

'I love you,' he said again. 'And now I'm going to show you just how much.'

He carried her over to the bed, and for the first time in his life he paid homage to a woman—his mouth deliciously brushing every centimetre of her soft, scented body. Suddenly, an act that he had performed countless times in his life—with predictable and pleasurable outcome—became something completely outside his experience. It felt as if he'd been catapulted into a brand-new dimension—like stepping into a place where colours were brighter and more intense, and everything somehow felt more *real*.

The joining together of their bodies felt so… *profound*…something so close to the spiritual that it almost defied description.

Afterwards, he felt the wetness of his tears mixed with hers. Only now he was discovering that you could cry for all kinds of reasons, and that these were tears of joy—and there was nothing wrong with *that*. Not in the sanctuary of the bedchamber, alone with this remarkable woman with whom he could be the man he could never be with anyone else.

He held her very tight and kissed her, and

then bent his mouth to her ear. 'I never want to let you go, Sorrel,' he said fiercely. 'My Queen, my wife, my lover.'

And Sorrel kissed the top of his tangled black head and hugged him back just as tightly, her heart burning with love for him.

EPILOGUE

SORREL sat before the mirror, brushing her hair until it hung heavy and free in a shimmering blonde curtain. She yawned. It had been a long evening—but a successful one. An evening to celebrate the opening of the first part of the new road which stretched from the capital all the way round to the western side of the country. One day it would reach as far as the beautiful mountains which divided Kharastan from the neighbouring country of Maraban. It would bring with it life and tourism—and the new jobs which were so needed in Kharastan—though there were those who opposed it.

'People always oppose progress, Sorrel,' Malik

had commented quietly, when she had relayed to him some of the rumblings of discontent she'd heard—mainly from visiting foreigners who wanted to keep the country to themselves, like a glorious undiscovered treasure.

'It's change they don't like,' she had replied thoughtfully.

'Well, that's always a stumbling block,' he agreed with a smile.

As a couple they'd had to cope with some big changes themselves—much more than the average newlyweds. The adjustment to married life. The getting used to living together. Sorrel's being thrown in at the deep end and learning how to be Queen. It was like being on a rollercoaster ride—dizzy and exciting and colourful, though occasionally exhausting.

To escape the exhaustion they had commissioned a leading Kharastani architect to build them a house on the Balsora Sea—a short distance away from where Xavier and Laura had their holiday home, and where Giovanni and Alexa were now looking to buy.

Their new house was full of the most amazing light, and the soothing sound of the nearby waves was better than a trip to any therapist! They were going there tomorrow, for the weekend, and Sorrel couldn't wait.

'Ah! You're still awake!'

Sorrel heard the satisfied voice of her husband, and Malik came to stand behind her, so that she saw his reflection in the mirror—his white robes shimmering—and leaned her head back against him.

'I always wait up for you,' she protested, and then murmured her pleasure as he began to massage her shoulders.

'I know you do, my angel.' He kissed the top of her head and then frowned. 'But I thought you looked tired tonight.'

How perceptive he had become, she thought lovingly. Yes, she *had* been tired, but there was a reason for that. 'A little.' She smiled, savouring the anticipation of telling him, and turned round, getting to her feet and putting her arms around his neck, her eyes soft as she looked at his beloved face. 'Remember you asked me to find your cufflinks? The ones that Giovanni and Alexa bought for your birthday last year?'

He lifted her hand and kissed the tips of her fingers. 'Mmm?'

'Well, I did. I found them in the back of the drawer in your dressing room.' She hesitated. 'And I found something else, too.'

'Oh?' He laughed. 'A secret?'

'Sort of.' She reached down to the dressing table and picked up a little box, held it up. It was a cheap little thing—covered in shells, with the word *Brighton* written on it. The kind of holiday souvenir that thousands of small children bought with their saved-up pocket money.

He looked at it, and then smiled. 'Ah.'

'*I*…bought you this, didn't I?' she affirmed tremblingly.

'Yes, you did, my darling. I think you must have been about ten.'

'And you kept it—all this time?'

Malik's eyes softened in a way he would once never have allowed them to—but he had learnt that it was okay to show his feelings to his wife, his beautiful and precious Sorrel.

'Yes, I kept it. It was the first real present I ever received.' He took it from her and turned it over thoughtfully in his hands, and then he looked at her. 'How appropriate that it should have come from you.'

There was a pause, and her heart pounded. 'I have…I have another present to give you,' she said softly. 'Something I think you might like even more.'

Malik's eyes narrowed as he stared at her blushing cheeks. Already he knew her so well, but every day was like a voyage of amazing discovery—and this soft, almost luminous Sorrel was one he hadn't seen before. 'Sorrel?'

Feeling suddenly shy, Sorrel lowered her

eyes, and when she lifted them to meet his she felt the glow of pride. 'I'm pregnant,' she whispered, meeting his incredulous look with a nod.

'You're going to have a baby?'

'Yes!' she said, and then started laughing. *'Yes!'*

They had both hoped for a baby, but it had been one of those wishes not really wished aloud—some primitive superstition making them think that would jinx it. Malik had never had a family of his own, and Sorrel's had been lost overnight, and this meant more to both of them than they would ever dare to admit.

'When?'

'I've only just found out…it's early days… but—'

He gave a whoop, and then a kind of proprietorial growl, as he put the box down and gathered her into his arms. 'You need to rest?' he demanded.

'No, darling.'

'You need to rest,' he said firmly, and

picked her up and carried her to the low divan beside the windows which overlooked the palace gardens.

'Yes, darling.' Sorrel smiled, thinking that she would let him have his way and then later she would give him her book on pregnancy to read— giving special attention to the chapter which included notes on 'How Not to Wrap the Pregnant Woman in Cotton Wool'. But just for now she would allow him to fuss over her. Because she could understand why he needed to.

This baby meant more to them than the continuance of a noble bloodline. In the end they were just the same as any other couple in love— and this baby was an expression of that love.

He sat at her feet and kissed her fingertips, and the sunshine illuminated the gleaming little shell-covered box—the only *real* present Malik had ever received, until Sorrel had grown up and come back and given him something more precious than the emeralds which were mined on the farthest reaches of his kingdom, or even than tiny shell boxes. The greatest gift of all.

The gift of love.

MILLS & BOON PUBLISH EIGHT LARGE PRINT TITLES A MONTH. THESE ARE THE EIGHT TITLES FOR SEPTEMBER 2007.

THE BILLIONAIRE'S SCANDALOUS MARRIAGE
Emma Darcy

THE DESERT KING'S VIRGIN BRIDE
Sharon Kendrick

ARISTIDES' CONVENIENT WIFE
Jacqueline Baird

THE PREGNANCY AFFAIR
Anne Mather

THE SHERIFF'S PREGNANT WIFE
Patricia Thayer

THE PRINCE'S OUTBACK BRIDE
Marion Lennox

THE SECRET LIFE OF LADY GABRIELLA
Liz Fielding

BACK TO MR & MRS
Shirley Jump

MILLS & BOON
Pure reading pleasure

0807 Rom LP

MILLS & BOON PUBLISH EIGHT LARGE PRINT TITLES A MONTH. THESE ARE THE EIGHT TITLES FOR OCTOBER 2007.

THE RUTHLESS MARRIAGE PROPOSAL
Miranda Lee

BOUGHT FOR THE GREEK'S BED
Julia James

THE GREEK TYCOON'S VIRGIN MISTRESS
Chantelle Shaw

THE SICILIAN'S RED-HOT REVENGE
Kate Walker

A MOTHER FOR THE TYCOON'S CHILD
Patricia Thayer

THE BOSS AND HIS SECRETARY
Jessica Steele

BILLIONAIRE ON HER DOORSTEP
Ally Blake

MARRIED BY MORNING
Shirley Jump

MILLS & BOON®
Pure reading pleasure

0907 Rom L